THE GOLDEN GIRL
AND ALL

THE GOLDEN GIRL AND ALL

RALPH DENNIS

BRASH
BOOKS

INTRODUCTION

Ralph Dennis and Hardman

By Joe R. Lansdale

Once upon the time there were a lot of original paperbacks, and like the pulps before them, they covered a lot of ground. Western, adventure, romance, mystery, science fiction, fantasy, and crime, for example.

There were also subsets of certain genres. One of those was the sexy, men's action-adventure novel with a dab of crime and mystery.

These books had suggestive titles, or indicators that not only were they action packed with blood and sweat, fists and bullets, but that there would be hot, wet sex. They were straight up from the male reader's perspective, the perspective of the nineteen seventies and early eighties.

There were entire lines of adult westerns for example. They sold well at the time. Quite well. These Westerns sold so well, that for a brief period it seemed as if it might go on forever. They made up the largest number of Westerns on the stands rivaled only by Louis L'Amour, and a few reprints from Max Brand and Zane Grey.

An agent once told me I was wasting my time writing other things, and I could be part of this big stable he had writing adult Westerns. Although I had nothing against sexy Westerns, which may in fact have been pioneered as a true branch of the Western genre by a very good writer named Brian Garfield and his novel *Sliphammer*, but I didn't want to spend a career writing them. Not the sort I had read, anyway.

Still, a small part of me, the part that was struggling to pay bills, thought maybe I could write something of that nature that might be good enough to put a pen name on. Many of my friends and peers were doing it, and some actually did it quite well, but if ever there was a formulaic brand of writing, that was it.

I was a big fan of Westerns in general, however, so I thought I might could satisfy that itch, while managing to satisfy the publisher's itch, not to mention that of the Adult Western reader, primarily males.

I picked up a number of the so called adult Westerns, read them, and even landed a job as a ghost for one series, but the publisher and the writer had a falling out, so my work was never published, though I got paid.

Actually, for me, that was the best-case scenario. Once I started on the series I knew I was in for trouble. It wasn't any fun for me, and that is the main reason I write. I woke up every morning feeling ill because I was trying to write that stuff. It was like trying to wear a tux to a tractor pull.

I thought, maybe there's something I would like more in the action-adventure line, crime, that sort of thing. I had read *The Executioner*, and had even written three in the *M.I.A. Hunter* series, and frankly, next to nailing my head to a burning building, I would rather have been doing anything else. But a look at our bank account made me more pliable.

But that was later. At the time I was looking at this sort of genre, trying to understand if there was anything in it I could truly like, I picked up a book by Ralph Dennis, *The Charleston Knife is Back in Town*, bearing the overall title of *Hardman*. The books were billed by the publisher as "a great new private eye for the shockproof seventies."

The title was suggestive in a non-subtle way, and I remember sighing, and cracking it open and hoping I could at least make it a third of the way through.

And then, it had me. It gripped me and carried me through, and one thing was immediately obvious. It wasn't a sex and shoot novel. It's not that those were not components, but not in the way of the other manufactured series, where sometimes the sex scenes were actually lifted from another one in the series and placed in the new one, in the perfunctory manner you might replace a typewriter ribbon.

I was working on a typewriter in those days, and so was everyone else. If that reference throws you, look it up. You'll find it somewhere between etched stone tablets and modern PCs.

Dennis wrote with assurance, and he built characterization through spot on first person narration. His prose was muscular, swift, and highly readable. There was an echo behind it.

Jim Hardman wasn't a sexy private eye with six-pack abs and face like Adonis. He was a pudgy, okay looking guy, and as a reader, you knew who Hardman was and how he saw things, including himself, in only a few pages.

You learned about him through dialogue and action. Dennis was good at both techniques. His action was swift and realistic, and you never felt as if something had been mailed in.

Hardman wasn't always likable, or good company. And he knew that about himself. He was a guy just trying to make it from day to day in a sweltering city. He had a friend named Hump, though Hardman was reluctant to describe him as such. In his view he and Hump were associates. He sometimes hired Hump to help him with cases where two men, and a bit of muscle, were needed.

That said, Hump was obviously important to Hardman, and as the series proceeded, he was more so. The books developed their world, that hot, sticky, Atlanta landscape, and it was also obvious that Dennis knew Atlanta well, or was at least able to give you the impression he did.

His relationship with Marcy, his girlfriend, had a convenient feel, more than that of a loving relationship, and it was off again and on again; it felt real, and the thing that struck me about the books was that there was real human fabric to them. There was action, of course, but like Chandler and Hammett before him, Dennis was trying to do something different with what was thought of as throw away literature.

I'm not suggesting Dennis was in the league of those writers, but he was certainly head and shoulders above the mass of paperbacks being put out fast and dirty. When I read Dennis's Hardman novels, the characters, the background, stayed with me. The stories were peripheral in a way. Like so many of the best modern crime stories, they were about character.

Due to the publishing vehicle and the purpose of the series, at least from the publisher's view point, the books sometimes showed a hastiness that undercut the best of the work, but, damn, I loved them. I snatched them up and devoured them.

I thought I might like to do something like that, but didn't, and a few years later I wrote those *M.I.A. Hunters*, which I actually loathed, and knew all my visitations with that branch of the genre I loved, crime and suspense, had ended, and not well, at least for me, though the three books were later collected and published in a hardback edition from Subterranean Press by me and its creator, Stephen Mertz.

A few years after that journey into the valley of death, quite a few, actually, I had a contract with Bantam, and I was trying to come up with a crime novel, and I wrote about this guy named Hap standing out in a field in East Texas, and with him, out of nowhere, was a gay, black guy named Leonard.

The idea of a black and white team in the depths of East Texas would be something I could write about, and it was a way for me to touch on social issues without having to make a parade of it. I thought, yeah, that'll work for me, and though my characters are quite different than Hardman, they share many similarities as well. The black and white team and Southern background (East Texas is more South than Southwestern), was certainly inspired by the Hardman novels. I think because it rang a bell with me, the clapper of that bell slapped up against my own personal experience, though mine was more rural than urban.

Even more than other writer heroes of mine, Chandler and Chester Himes for example, Hardman spoke directly to me. Chandler's language and wise cracks fit the people I grew up with, and Himes wrote about the black experience, something that was vital to the South, though often given a sideways consideration and the back of culture's hand. But Hardman had that white blue collar feel, even if he was in the city and was already an established, if unlicensed, private investigator and thug for hire. I blended all those writers, and many more, to make Hap and Leonard, John D. McDonald, certainly, but if I had a spirit guide with the Hap and Leonard books, it was Ralph Dennis.

So now we have the Hardman books coming back into print.

I am so excited about this neglected series being brought back, put in front of readers again. It meant a lot to me back then, and it still means a lot. You can beef about the deficiency of political correctness, but twenty years from now they'll be beefing about our lack of political correctness on some subject or another that we now think we are hip to. And too much political correctness is the enemy of truth, and certainly there are times when fiction is not about pretty manners but should ring the true bells of social conditions and expression. Erasing what is really going on, even in popular fiction, doesn't do anyone any favors. Righteous political correctness has its place, but political correct police do not.

I know very little about Ralph Dennis. I know this. He wrote other books outside the Hardman series. I don't think he had the career he deserved. The Hardman books were a product of their time, but they managed to be about their time, not of it. They stand head and shoulders above so much of the paperback fodder that was designed for men to hold the book in one hand, and something else in the other. And I don't mean a can of beer.

But one thing is for sure, these books are still entertaining, and they are a fine time capsule that addresses the nature and attitudes of the time in which they were written. They do that with clean, swift prose, sharp characterization, and an air of disappointment in humanity that seems more and more well-earned.

I'm certainly glad I picked that Hardman novel up those long years ago. They were just what I needed. An approach that imbedded in my brain like a knitting needle, mixed with a variety of other influences, and helped me find my own voice. An authentic Southern voice. A voice that wasn't that of New York or Los Angeles or Chicago, but a voice of the South.

Thanks Ralph Dennis for helping me recognize that my background was as good a fodder for popular fiction as any, and that popular fiction could attempt to rise above the common crime novel. I don't know that I managed that, but Ralph Dennis was one of those writers that made me try.

Dennis may not have made literature of Hardman, but he damn sure touched on it more than a time or two, and I wish you the joy I got from first reading these novels, so many long, years ago.

Read on.

PUBLISHER'S NOTE

This book was originally published in 1974 and reflects the cultural and sexual attitudes, language, and politics of the period.

CHAPTER ONE

The Early Bird flight from Atlanta to New York touched
down at Raleigh-Durham airport at 6:59 A.M. There were
twenty-eight passengers in the tourist section and eleven in first
class. Only three passengers debarked at Raleigh-Durham. They
moved down the ramp in single file and walked the hundred
yards or so across the apron to the gate and through the gate into
the terminal proper. It was January 15th, a Monday, and the land
around the airport showed the damage from the ice storm that
had blanketed the southeast a week before.

One of the three was a girl in her mid-twenties with pale,
luminous skin and long flowing black hair that almost reached
her waist. She wore a gray tweed pants suit and black boots. She
didn't seem aware of it but now and then she hitched the pants
up and tugged at the shoulders of the jacket, as if the fit wasn't
quite right.

In the main concourse of the terminal she paused just long
enough to get her bearings and then she headed for the Hertz
booth. There she presented a Master Charge card and rented a
Mustang. Before she went outside to wait for the Mustang, she
stopped at the Eastern ticket counter to confirm a return flight.

The Mustang was waiting for her in the loading-unloading
area and she drove past the outdoor baggage shelf where the two
men who'd debarked with her waited impatiently, chilled, for
their luggage. Where the airport exit road touched the highway
she paused long enough to locate the sign that read CHAPEL
HILL. She drove the distance in just a bit over half an hour. At

7:48 she was driving through the center of downtown Chapel Hill. It was cold and windy and the only human movement she saw on the street was in front of Jeff's Campus Confectionary, where a swarthy, balding man was lifting huge bales of newspapers from the sidewalk and carrying them inside.

She seemed in no special hurry. She continued out Franklin street until she passed Spencer dorm on her right and, using that as a landmark, she turned left onto Pittsboro Road and followed this winding road until she reached the Madison Apartments. She slowed then and turned left under the archway and traced the figure-eight road that snaked through the colonial fronted apartment complex. At apartment 42A she'd slowed to about five miles an hour. She looked at the curtained windows and the Ford station wagon out front. Then, as if on a strong impulse, she u-turned and drove out of the apartment complex at an ever increasing speed.

At twenty to nine, she'd been parked in the unloading zone in front of the Estes Hills Elementary School for ten minutes. In the next five minutes, the traffic increased, the mothers and fathers dropping their children off and watching them scamper through the entrance. At thirteen to nine, she checked her watch and looked down the road in both directions. The traffic was thinning. But the woman covered the watch with her sleeve and continued to wait. At ten to nine the Ford station wagon turned into the driveway. The woman behind the wheel wore a scarf over tangled, uncombed hair and a light camel hair coat over slacks and a sweater. As soon as she braked the station wagon, she reached across the little girl next to her and pushed the door open. The little girl got out quickly and gave the door a push. It closed but it didn't lock and the woman, impatient and seemingly in a hurry, opened the door once more and pulled it shut with a heavy slam. Then, without looking at the little girl, she pulled away from the curb.

The little girl was six going on seven and tall for her age, but very thin. Her dark hair was pulled back into a ponytail and tied with a red ribbon. She wore red, knee-length stockings and a short black dress under a red wool coat. She stood at the curb for a moment and watched the station wagon move away. For a second it looked as if she might wave, but the hand didn't go all the way up. She was turning and heading for the school entrance when she heard a car pull up behind and stop. The child turned and saw the woman who'd been waiting in the unloading zone. The woman slid across the seat to the passenger side and opened the car door.

"Maryann," the woman said, "it's me. Don't you know me?"

At first it was surprise and shock but that gave way to happiness. "Yes, yes, I know you."

The girl ran to the woman and hugged her. The woman whispered to her for a moment and the little girl got into the Mustang and the woman closed the door and pushed the lock button down.

At 9:55 the Eastern Whisperjet to Atlanta left Raleigh-Durham. The young woman and the little girl sat next to each other on the outside seats in the tourist section. The little girl cried part of the time and the woman with her cried too. The stewardess in their section was concerned at first but there were so many things to do on the short flight that she lost interest in them when she saw, a few minutes later, that they were calm again. It was, she decided, the first flight for the little girl.

I was in the bathroom shaving when the phone rang in the bedroom. It was a cold January morning and I had a feeling that the furnace was about to give its death rattle. If that happened I'd have to find a place to stay for a few days while they put in another one. I wasn't sure that Marcy would take me in for that long. That meant that Hump might have to, even if that cut down on his round-robin circus of sweetmeat trim.

I got the phone on the third ring.

"Hardman? This is Jack Smathers. Remember me?"

For a brief moment I didn't. I seemed to have gone blank. He helped me out. "I was on the D.A.'s staff a few years back."

"Sure." It came back to me. Jack was a young guy then, just out of University of Georgia law school, hungry as hell and with a pair of ears like a jack rabbit. He'd prosecuted a few cases I'd done the work on and a couple of times I'd taken him out for a few drinks afterwards.

"You busy right now?" he asked.

"Nothing I know of," I said.

"Can you come by my office … in say, an hour?"

I checked my watch on the night stand next. It was right around ten o'clock. "Money in this or is it old home week?"

"Money … not much but your usual. At least what Art Maloney said was your usual."

I took down his address and said I'd be there at eleven on the dot.

Jack Smathers' office was in one of those old buildings on Forsyth Street, one of the few that hasn't been torn down to put up a new seventy floor hotel or a new office skyscraper. The entrance was through a staircase that ran right beside the Mellow Mood Bar, a place where at least half the day laborers from the area's labor contractors cashed their checks and drank their beer. It wasn't an impressive address.

The hallway had almost no lighting and the narrow strip of carpet didn't do much to deaden the squeaking board floor. I found Jack's office and knocked and then pushed on in. There was a blonde girl behind the desk in the outer office and she looked like typing the whereases and the therefores had about rotted her mind. I gave her my name and watched as she got up and walked over to the door of the closed inner office. I got a good look at the rest of the machinery and I realized that it didn't matter if brain rot got that part of her. The rest of her was going to be good for some years to come.

She was gone just a few seconds. She came back and gave me the high grade dazzling smile. "You can go on in, Mr. Hardman."

I did. I knew Jack Smathers right away. He might have gotten a little older and he might have moved up to a better suit than the one he'd bought himself for graduation and job hunting. And he might have decided to wear his hair a bit fashionably long. But there wasn't anything he could do with those jack rabbit years short of surgery. I knew I could pick him out of a crowd of 58,000 any Sunday at a Falcon game.

The man with him was a few years younger than Jack and a hell of a lot younger than I was. He was in his mid to late twenties and he had that Ivy League tailoring look. Something vaguely Joe College in his dress and his manner. Oh, it was all proper and very neat but it wasn't quite the business world yet. He had dark hair and an intense look on his almost girlishly slim face.

Jack motioned me to a chair. "This is Edward Simpson, Jim."

I got a touch from the hand. It was a strong hand, but not a working hand. It was more like a tennis hand or a handball hand.

"Mr. Simpson's got a problem," Jack said. "He has reason to believe that his ex-wife kidnapped his little girl and has her somewhere in Atlanta."

I looked at Jack and then over at Simpson. "Maybe you need the police rather than me."

"It's a bit more complicated than that," Simpson said. And right away I didn't like him. It was that slightly patronizing smile that meant I wasn't to be offended if he had to show me up for the half-wit that I so obviously was. "In fact, it's going to be rather difficult any way we handle it at all."

I looked over at Jack. Simpson wasn't making much sense to me and I knew that, while Jack could spread dust and fog with the best of them in the courtroom, he'd been raised on a farm and if you asked him for a good country answer he could usually come up with one that even I could understand.

"Mr. Simpson and his wife were divorced almost three years ago," Jack said. "The little girl, Maryann, was around three then."

"A few months past three," Simpson said.

"The custody of the child was awarded to her mother at the time of the divorce. Two years ago he received a call from Atlanta. His ex-wife was in trouble and needed help. And she needed someone to take care of Maryann."

"What kind of trouble?" I asked.

"A drug bust. Down in the tight squeeze area. Not at her apartment but the place of a friend. Tabs of acid in the refrigerator and about a pound of grass."

"I came down as quickly as I could," Simpson said. "And I arranged for a lawyer to defend her."

Jack grinned at me. That meant he'd been the lawyer.

"At the time it looked like Margaret might get a big jail sentence and she wanted me to take care of Maryann. In fact, she was so upset that she as much as told me that she wanted me to have custody of Maryann ... for good."

Jack said, "Mr. Simpson has remarried, so there was no question about the kind of home he could give the child."

"What do you do?" I asked Simpson.

"I'm finishing up my Ph.D. at North Carolina ... in English. To tell the truth, this has come up at rather a bad time. I'm due to take my written exams in less than a week."

"At his ex-wife's request, Mr. Simpson took Maryann back to North Carolina," Jack said. "But, Mr. Simpson neglected to follow through on some good legal advice I gave him."

"I made a mistake," Simpson said, "but the pressure of the degree program ..."

Jack cut him off. "Since the divorce was granted in Orange county in North Carolina, I advised him to go to court immediately and sue for custody of Maryann. Under the circumstances, the trial and such, I thought he had a very good chance of getting full legal custody."

"What happened to the ex-wife?

Jack grinned and me. "She had a very good lawyer and she got off as a first offender with a year's probation."

"That was two years ago?" I asked.

Simpson nodded.

"Have you heard from or seen her since then?"

"She called Maryann several times and once she came up to Chapel Hill for a few days and spent hours at a time with Maryann."

"Did she say anything about wanting the child back?"

"Not in so many words. But I could see that she did. I guess she knew I wouldn't let her have Maryann without a court fight."

"At any rate," Jack said, "yesterday morning she picked up the child from in front of the elementary school in Chapel Hill and we think she flew down here with her."

"You check it out?"

"A Mrs. Margaret Simpson and a Maryann Simpson were on the passenger list of a flight that landed here in Atlanta yesterday around eleven A.M."

"You know where she lives?"

"That's our problem," Jack said. "We spent all of yesterday afternoon trying to find her through all of the usual ways. So far no luck."

"You tried phones, gas, electric, water?"

"All those," Jack said.

"Then she's changed her name or she's living with somebody," I said.

"That's it. Something like that. You think you can find her, Jim?"

"Maybe." I got up and stretched and looked at Jack and then at Simpson. "What happens if I find her? You kidnap her and take her back to North Carolina?"

Jack shook his head. "That's what Mr. Simpson wants me to let him do. I don't think I can go along with that and stay in the Georgia Bar Association very long. So I've convinced him that this kidnap nonsense could go on for years if we don't get it settled once and for all. We want you to find them so that we can institute a suit for custody."

"I'll find them if they're still in town," I said. "That and just that. I won't dig dirt for you to sue on."

"That was never a part of the deal," Jack said. "Fifty a day?"

"And some expenses."

"How long?"

"If she's been on drugs and still is, there'll be ways to find her." I thought about it a moment. "That way two or three days at the most. If she's quit drugs it'll take longer. Maybe a week."

"You need an advance?"

I shook my head. Most of the time I'd insist upon an advance. Some of the time it was the only way to be sure I'd get paid. But I knew Jack and it didn't seem necessary. Also I had a major part of the loot we'd made off with during our intrusion into the J.C. Cartway fight-robbery thing still left. It was socked away in a shoebox in the back of my closet. That gave me a kind of independence that I liked. If I found I didn't like this one I could always call Jack and tell him I was through with it. If I hadn't taken his money he wouldn't have any real bitch with me. "I'll turn in my bill later."

"Hold the expenses down," Jack said.

I nodded at him and saw the trace of a grin. That was for the benefit of Simpson. So I decided that I'd go along with it. "Sometimes I have to buy information."

"Buy from the small-timers," he said.

All that didn't seem to impress Simpson at all. He was staring at his watch and looking bored. He got up and moved around his chair and stood with his hands on the back of the chair. "If you think it will take two or three days there's no reason for me to stay in town. I can be back within three hours of hearing from you."

"Fine," Jack said. He got up and I remained seated. He gave me a questioning look.

"I need a few more facts," I said.

Jack went out of the office with Simpson and I could hear him out in the waiting room telling Simpson that I was the best around, at any money, and we were very lucky they'd found me when I wasn't busy. He also said that as soon as I found the mother and Maryann he'd start custody proceedings. At that time, he'd need another check from Simpson. Simpson said he'd have to deposit some more money in his checking account and that he would wait and write the check the next time he was in town.

Jack saw him out the door and came back into his office shaking his head. He nodded in the direction of Simpson's chair. "Fucking idiot. Couldn't do what I told him to."

"Impressed me as an asshole too," I said.

"Thought he might." Jack stood behind his desk. "What do you need from me?"

"More facts on the girl. A better run-down. The kind you might not want to give me in front of the ex-husband."

"Didn't remember you being this delicate." Jack went over to the file cabinet in the corner of the room and got out a folder. He brought it back to the desk and sat down and opened it.

"A picture of the ex-wife?"

Jack reached into the desk drawer on his left and brought out a snapshot. "It's not a recent one," he said. He passed it to me.

The girl was seated on a bench. It was probably on a campus somewhere. The building in the background seemed to belong on college or university grounds. She was a pretty girl and she wore her hair in a pageboy cut. She looked out at the camera with a solemn, unfriendly look.

"What's different?"

"When I defended her, the hair was longer, far down her back. The face is thinner now, all the baby fat gone and she doesn't wear make-up now, so she might seem plainer."

"I doubt that." I put the photo in the breast pocket of my jacket.

"What else?"

"Everything you know about her." I got out a pad and a squirreled a pen from the front of Jack's desk.

"Born in Reedsville, North Carolina on December 14th, 1947. That makes her twenty-five now. Father a dentist. Mother dead. Started at Women's College at Greensboro ... that's U.N.C. at Greensboro now. Was seventeen when she entered. Was going to major in comparative literature. Her sophomore year met the idiot boy, Edward Simpson, at a party in Chapel Hill. Married him within a couple of months. Over Christmas vacation, I think. Dropped out of Women's college and moved into student housing, got a job somewhere on campus. The child, Maryann, was born the following September." He looked over at me. "You don't have to count it on your fingers. I think she got pregnant the first time they screwed."

"Likely," I said.

"It went well for a time. About two years to be exact. Then Margaret got involved with another man, another graduate student named Hansen. From what Simpson said, this Hansen was a real fuck-up. A guy who was into grass and L.S.D. One of the types who never seemed to finish their degrees. Just hang around college towns forever. So, one day Margaret took the little girl and moved out on Edward and right into Hansen's apartment."

"What did Simpson do about this?"

"From what he said, very little. He just waited out the year and got a divorce on the one-year separation grounds."

"And right after that she moved to Atlanta?"

"Almost on the same day the divorce was granted," Jack said.

"With or without Hansen?"

"Without, from what Simpson said. Just her and the kid."

"When she was busted, was she living alone or with somebody?"

"Living with a guy named Al Connor. Worked with the state welfare department."

"Was he busted too?"

Jack shook his head. "She'd gone to the other apartment without him. In fact, he didn't know where she'd gone."

"Ready to dump him too, huh?"

"Might be," Jack said.

"Where was she living then?"

Jack checked the folder and gave me an address on Eleventh Street. I wrote it down. "You see her after the trial?"

"What kind of question is that?"

"Well," I said, grinning at him, "it wasn't much of a question when I first asked it, but it's getting better all the time."

"You bastard," he said.

"So you were doing her too?"

He shrugged. "It was hard not to."

"How long?"

"A week or two," he said. "It started right after I got her off. Maybe women clients get a thing for their lawyers the way they fall in love with their psychiatrists."

"What happened?"

"I really don't know. Nothing I know of. One day it was good and the next day it wasn't."

"Any guesses?"

"The one I guess a man always makes in a situation like that," he said.

"Another man?"

"That's what I thought."

"You check it out?" I asked.

"Of course not." He sounded offended.

"Come on, Jack. You're a fact person. You'd check it out until you knew for sure. You couldn't stand not being sure."

"The day after she chopped me a guy moved in with her."

"Where was she living then?"

"The same place on Eleventh Street."

"What happened to Al Connor?"

"I don't know," Jack said. "He moved out while the trial was going on."

"Who was the guy moved in with her?"

"I don't know. That's the truth. Something of a hood. Real hard looking kind of a guy."

"You ever see her again?"

He shook his head. "I wrote it off. Called it pussy and tried to treat it that way."

"Liked her, huh?"

"She's quite a girl. It's hard to talk about but there was something in her … well, it's just hard …" There was a kind of choked quality to his voice and that told me the rest of it.

I decided to let it go. "What kind of work can she do?"

"She was working at Rich's until the drug bust. After that I'm not sure. She was getting support from Simpson. Worked for a time at one of the hip dress shops down on the Strip, around the tight squeeze area."

"Which one?"

"Some kind of unisex place. Not sure what that means. Not sure which one. Must be five or six of them down there."

I put the pad in my pocket. "How's Simpson with money?"

"His second wife had a bit of a bundle. I'm not sure how she feels about the way he's spending it, but so far the purse is open."

"I'd like to use Hump Evans on this. He knows some people I don't and he can ask some questions I can't. With him maybe I can cut the time down."

"All right. I don't think Simpson'll bitch. If he does I'll run it into my fee and pay Hump out of that."

"I'll see if I can find him." I went to the door and opened it.

"Keep in touch," Jack said.

I couldn't resist it. I turned back to him. "How's your wife, Jack?"

"Ignorant of all this," he said.

I nodded and went past the blonde secretary. Giving her my goodbye look I wondered what else May Smathers was ignorant of.

CHAPTER TWO

Hump didn't answer his phone. Just on a guess I drove over to the Westend Health Spa. The last couple of months he'd been working out there regularly. I'd tried once or twice to find out why he'd gone that routine after years of seeming not to worry about it. So far all his answers were evasive

The attendant said yes, Mr. Evans was in. He'd send word back right away. It was a twenty minute wait during which I had a hell of a time convincing the attendant that I wasn't interested in a trial membership, not even ten visits at a dollar a visit. He said some fine words about "getting back in shape" as if he believed that once I had been.

Hump came out looking polished and buffed. He'd spent some of his windfall from the J.C. Cartway fight-robbery on some new threads. He was wearing a maroon and white striped double-knit jacket and a pair of sky-blue flared pants. The black boots looked like glove leather.

I gave him a long up and down look. I didn't say anything. Hump waved at the attendant and came over to me. "What's up, Jim?"

"Too early for a beer?"

"No."

We stopped out in front of the Spa, in the center of the parking lot. "And I've worked up an appetite, too," Hump said.

We settled on the Fisherman's Inn, a place about a mile from the Spa. Hump tailgated me all the way over there.

I sipped a beer and watched Hump work through two dozen raw oysters. He was down to the last two when I finished spreading the job offer out for him. He shook a dot of Tabasco on the center of each oyster and capped the bottle.

"You short of money already, Jim?"

"Not yet." I grinned at him. "Didn't spend my money on fancy duds."

"Wouldn't fit you anyway," Hump said.

"It's not the money, so I guess I'm bored. Sleeping late gets old fast and after I'm up it's a matter of counting time until the first drink. After that it's downhill."

Hump took up the last two oysters, one in each hand, and sucked them from the half-shell. He chewed for a moment. "Your problem, Jim, is that you got to get rid of that white middle-class work ethic shit before it's too late."

"Boredom," I said.

"You could come down to the Spa and work out with me."

"I'd drop dead in the steam room."

"Why this job?" Hump asked.

"It's the only one offered me."

"We could do a trip to New York," Hump said. "Some real sweetmeat trim up there."

I shook my head. "I called Raymond a few days ago and checked. No need for one right now. Seems, from the code he was talking, that the street's overflowing with the shit now. Raymond doesn't know where it's coming from. And the quality's high."

"That could be blood in the street."

"Maybe," I said, "or just some ass kicking."

Hump pushed the plate of shells away and put his elbows on the table. "This job's small shit. Two days work. Maybe not even that." He gave me a hard-eyed look. "You care one way or the other about the little girl? About whether the father or the mother gets her?"

RALPH DENNIS

"Not really. I'm just guessing but I think both of them are losers. The kid stays with the mother and she'll have clap at sixteen and a coke-sniffing spoon of her own. The father's that bad, but in the other direction. The right schools and a big coming-out and the good marriage. That makes me as sick as the clap at sixteen and the coke spoon."

"A stand-off," Hump said. He waved past me at the waiter and the waiter brought over two more beers and huge bowl of boiled shrimp in the shells. "You keep talking like that, Hardman, and I'm going to make you an honorary nigger."

"I might accept," I said. I got the first reach into the bowl and brought out a big one. I peeled it and dipped it in the Fishermen's Inn's special fiery sauce. "It's the usual. Fifty a day and some expenses. You're on the payroll today if you're interested."

Hump popped a shrimp into his mouth and gave me that easy grin. "To tell the truth, I'm a little bored myself. Could wish there was more loot in it, but I guess we can't change that."

"You're a sly fucker," I said. "You were just waiting to be asked to the dance."

"Now you got it, Hardman. Now you got it."

I paid the tab and followed Hump to the pay phone over by the front entrance. I watched over his shoulder as he dialed. "Ernie, this is Hump." He listened for a few seconds. "Look, can I stop by for a few minutes?" He swung his head and looked at me. "Just need a favor, Ernie. I'm going to bring a friend with me. Name's Jim Hardman." Hump dipped one eyelid at me. "Sure, he's cool, no problem there. Fifteen or twenty minutes then."

He hung up and we went outside. We walked over to his car. "Who's Ernie?"

"The Wildwood connector," he said.

"The what?"

"The Wildwood connector. Sells high grade grass and hash. No hard stuff." He nodded over at my car. "Lock it and we'll pick it up after our visit."

16

"It's locked." I went around and got in. It was a cold bleak day, not the best kind of day to begin anything. Maybe it didn't mean anything. I just felt like it did.

"That call back there," Hump said, "is part of the routine for a buy from Ernie." He worked his way out of the lot and pushed himself into the early afternoon traffic. "You call and ask if you can stop by. If Ernie says yes, the buy's possible. If he says he's going out or something like that it means he thinks a narc might be around or he doesn't have the stuff."

"He owe you for anything?"

"Not a thing. If he knows anything it might cost you twenty or so of that expense money."

"As long as it's good information."

"If the Simpson broad is still in dope he'll know her or he'll know somebody who does."

It was an old white frame house on Eleventh between Piedmont and Peachtree. There was one odd thing about it: somebody'd poured concrete where the lawn should have been. Now the "lawn" was a parking lot. Hump swung in and parked next to the only car there, a '72 Pinto. I started to get out but Hump stopped me.

"I better talk to him a minute or two. I've got a feeling he might have heard you were a cop once. If he's still nervous I'll have him call Raymond for an okay on you."

I smoked a cigarette and waited. Hump was inside about five minutes before he came out on the porch and waved me inside. I followed Hump up a long flight of stairs to the second floor. At the top of the stairs, the landing led to a single door. Hump was in front and he pushed the door open. On the way past the door I turned and looked at it. It was about three inches thick and looked solid. There were some steel brackets on it about waist high and I made my guess they were designed to hold an iron cross-bar. It was, I thought, one way of making his place rip-off proof.

It was a large living room. The furniture was mismatched and old, like it had been ordered by phone from a Goodwill store. Still, it had a good feel to it. The walls had been given a new coat of white paint recently and the framed prints, mostly the Impressionists, had been selected with some care.

Ernie was a black with a neat goatee and long sideburns that ran all the way down his face and joined the goatee. I put his age at around thirty, give or take a year or two. He was wearing a pair of navy bells and a flowing white silk shirt with wide sleeves.

That was the first impression. Then Ernie nodded at us and got up from the sofa. As he walked toward the kitchen, off to the right, I saw that he was dragging his right leg. I looked over at Hump but he didn't say anything. The leg didn't mean anything to him, but it did to me. I'd been around narcotics enough to know a dirty-needle-fucked-up leg when I saw one. If it was that I gave him about a year before they'd have to take it off.

Ernie came back from the kitchen with a quart of Dud and some plastic cups. He saw me looking at the leg. "Made your guess, huh, Hardman?"

I shook my head.

"You'd be wrong," he said. "Nam about six years ago."

"I did the Korean one," I said. "That one didn't make much sense either."

He nodded. His face didn't change. I felt a little foolish for throwing the Korean one into it. It didn't give us any rapport and there was always the chance that he'd think I was sucking up to him. I hoped that he wouldn't, but if he did there wasn't much I could do about it.

"You call Raymond?" Hump asked.

Ernie split the quart of beer three ways. He handed two of them to Hump and Hump passed me one. "Wouldn't call anybody on my home phone. Wouldn't trust those pigs out there not to have a tap on it." Ernie tongued at the foam and eyed me. "I've known Hump for two or three years. I guess I can trust him not to set me up." He winked at Hump. "Anyway there's not a flake of smoke in the place."

Ernie'd taken his seat back on the sofa and Hump was sitting next to him. I'd taken the stuffed chair at the end of the sofa nearest Ernie.

"Who's this cunt you two are asking about?"

"Margaret Simpson. Been in Atlanta about three years. One drug bust two years ago. Got a year's probation on that. Still living here we think and might be somewhere down here on the Strip."

"Name's nothing to me," Ernie said.

I got out the photo I'd gotten from Jack Smathers. I passed it to him. "The picture goes back a few years. Her hair's probably longer now."

He nodded a couple of times as he studied the photo. "I know this fuck. Did her a few times myself." He passed the picture back to me. "She doesn't go by that name anymore." He looked away from me, toward Hump. "You said something about expense money. You got twenty-five on you?"

Hump dipped his head toward me. I got out a ten and three fives. He didn't put out a hand for the money so I placed it on the table next to the empty quart bottle. His eyes flicked down at the cash but he didn't touch it.

"Why do you want to find her. Is she in any trouble with the law?"

"No," I said. "It's a custody suit over a six-year-old child. I'm working for a lawyer who wants to find her so he can serve her with notice of the suit."

"A child?"

"A little girl," I said.

"She needs a kid like she needs another A-hole."

"It's just hunt and find and the court does the rest," I said.

"Just wanted to be sure," Ernie said. "I sell grass and hash, but I don't usually sell people."

"What's the name now?" Hump asked.

"Peggy's short for Margaret, ain't it? She goes by that front name now. Last name's Holt. Don't know where that comes from."

"How can we find her?"

"I haven't seen her in three months or so. I had my thing with her about a year and a half ago. She's one crazy fuck. Like a lot of that white meat, needs a lot of dope to turn it all loose." He cut his eyes toward me to see how I reacted to all that, but I just shrugged. "About three months ago I went into one of those topless places between Tenth and Eleventh. A joint called Eve's Place. Just went in to see if titty still looked the same. There she was working as a waitress. Not dancing, just waiting the tables. I heard later she and the manager, a guy named Martin, had a thing going. Seems she had been doing some dancing, caught Martin's eye, and he retired her from dancing. Didn't want everybody looking at his property, I guess. I didn't hear this from Peggy. She brought me a beer and looked right through me."

"Think she's still there?" I asked.

"Maybe," he said.

"You find out where she was living then?"

He gave me a fuck-you grin. "Didn't ask. But assumed it was with this Martin guy. Of course, with the itch Peggy's got she might have moved on by now."

"What itch is that?"

"Man itch. Money itch. You take your choice. It might sound funny but fucking and money are tied together for that girl."

"She selling it?" Hump asked.

"Not out front," Ernie said. "Not that way. All the same it's got a price tag on it. One you might not read from close up. It's there, though."

I finished my beer and nodded at Hump. Hump tapped his plastic cup on the coffee table top and stood up. "Appreciate it, Ernie."

"Come by again. Got some real good Georgia mountain stuff coming in the next few days. It's got a mule's kick."

"I'll do it," Hump said.

Before I reached the door Ernie called after me. "Hardman?"

"Yeah."

"The reason I went to so much trouble to find out why you wanted to find Peggy ... you wonder about that?"

"I noticed it," I said.

"Heard a story a week or so ago. A rumor about that cunt. Heard she's dealing in hard stuff now. Good shit and lots of it. Raymond's boys are asking around. I wanted to make sure you weren't working for him."

"You didn't tell Raymond?"

"All that hard talking shit about Peggy. Part of that's a lie. I might have got ripped off by her, but I don't hate her enough to turn her into dogmeat."

"Raymond won't hear it from me."

He gestured down at the money I'd put on the table. "You wonder why I settled on twenty-five?"

"I thought you needed a new shirt," I said.

"If it was blood money I didn't want it to be thirty," he said.

"You think Raymond's after blood?"

"Doubt it," he said. "Think he's more interested in where she got it. The purity's high."

"How much of it is there?"

"No way to know without asking Peggy."

"Thanks, Ernie," I said.

"For what, man? Selling her ass out?"

Going out the door I took one more look at him. He was looking down at the cash. He still hadn't touched it. The Judas metaphor of his hadn't worked too well with me. Still, I guess that was the way he felt. He wanted to sell her ass out and at the same time he didn't want her hurt. It was a confusion of sorts but then love usually is.

On the way down the stairs I thought about Peggy Holt. I'd talked to two men who'd been in her bed, not counting the ex-husband, and they both sounded like the barbed fish hooks were still in.

Peggy Holt, more than anything else, sounded like yellow fever with a crotch.

CHAPTER THREE

hadn't admitted it back at Ernie's house, but I knew very well where Eve's Place was. Back in a dreary time, when the Marcy thing hadn't been going well, I'd gone in there a few times. Like Ernie had said, just to see what a breast and a butt looked like. It turned out to be a bit more than that. I got a little foolish and found myself attracted to one of the girls who danced there. A little blonde child named Fay. I guess if I'd had any sense I'd have known better. I finally realized that she'd been measuring my bankroll and trying to guess how much of it she could make off with without having to go to bed with me. And about the same time I got that realization I saw her talking to a scraggly-bearded kid at the door and I knew that the kid was probably her husband or the guy she was living with and supporting. That seemed to be one of the hard facts down there: most of the topless dancers seemed to be hustling money for some guy. And getting it from some forty-year-old fish like me.

As far as I could discover, there wasn't anybody named Eve connected with the place. It was just a way of explaining the concept, the design, of the bar. It was an almost square room. In the center of it was an apple-shaped raised platform where the girls danced. All around the apple-shaped platform were barstools where the customers who wanted to get close would sit. The stem of the apple was a runway that ran to a window at the rear of the bar where the dancers would get beers or drinks for the customers. The outer edges of the room were dotted with small two-person tables: A customer sat there if he didn't want to smell the powder and the sweat.

Hump and I took a table on the left side of the apple stage. It was early yet but there were thirty or so men in the place watching the four girls do their all-night shuffle to rock music that was set about one decibel below ear-ripping.

A waitress found us before the chair bottoms were warm. A young girl with long black hair and horn-rimmed glasses, a dancer whose turn it was to wait the tables, danced over to us. She didn't stop wiggling the whole time. I guess she'd become good at lip-reading because she nodded when I said, "Two Buds," and she danced all the way to the bar.

"Is Martin in?" I asked her when I paid her for the beers.

"He's in back," she said.

"I'd like to see him."

"Go on back," she said and she pointed to a hallway at the end of the aisle on the right side of the stage. She danced away and Hump and I got up and went down the aisle past the juke box. At the end of the short hall there was an open door. The man behind the desk watched us the whole way. He looked more like his name had been Martinez or something like that—Cuban or Spanish blood in him. He was seated but from what I could see of him he looked slim and hard.

"What can I do for you?" He spoke as soon as we were through the doorway.

"Mind if we close the door? I'm already half deaf and I've only been here five minutes."

He nodded and I closed the door. I gave him my name and introduced Hump to him. He didn't offer to shake hands. He had a large sheaf of file cards in his hands and he kept fanning them out and closing them into a stack.

"There was a Jim Hardman who was a cop once. That you?"

"That's me."

"You busted a friend of mine for armed robbery. He was innocent."

"So many innocent people in the slam I wonder why they keep building prisons," I said. He hadn't offered us a chair but I went over and sat in the one over to the left of the desk. "What was your innocent friend's name?"

"Art Conway."

"I didn't come here to talk about Conway." Of course I did remember Art Conway. It was hard not to. "You ought to pick your innocent friends better. Conway's the worst fuck-up thief in Atlanta. Can't even rob a poor box without tripping an alarm."

Martin didn't like that. "He's getting out a month or so from now. He'll probably come looking for you."

I grinned at him. "That's nothing to worry about. Conway couldn't find me even with a road map."

Hump hooted at that and I guess Martin decided that he wasn't winning the word game. "You come here just to waste my time?"

"I'm doing a skip-trace on a girl used to work here for you," I said.

"That's a comedown from being a big cop," Martin said.

I let that float by. "Her real name's Margaret Simpson."

"I don't know any Margaret Simpson."

"I think you knew her as Peggy Holt." I'd been watching his face. He hadn't reacted to Margaret Simpson, but Peggy Holt drew a hard line across his mouth.

"That dog."

"That's the one," I said. "She still working for you?"

"I fired her a few weeks ago. Got so she was missing her shift and coming in late."

"You know where she's living now?"

"I don't keep books on that dog," he said.

"Make a guess," I said.

"Not me. You might ask the blonde with the fried egg tits. They were close at one time. She might know."

I didn't remember a blonde that fitted that description. "She on now?"

He checked his watch. "She's due now." He gave me a bored look. "Is that all you want?"

I got up and swung the chair back into place with the toe of my shoe. "You've been just great."

"Hardman, you really get far down on your luck, I could use a bouncer here."

It was an insult but not a very good one. "If I ever get that hard up I'll stop by."

We sat at our table and finished our beers. I didn't have much trouble finding the blonde who fitted Martin's crude metaphor. She was a big horse woman. The waitress danced over to us again and reached us about the time the record ended. There was a silent space about long enough for me to get a few words in. I ordered two more beers and put an extra dollar on her tray. "The big blonde there. I'd like to talk to her. It's business. Five in it for her."

"I'll talk to you for five," the waitress said.

"This is business," I said. "Talking to you would be pleasure."

"If she wants to come, she'll be over when her set's finished."

"What's her name?"

"Ellen."

The sound blast of music started up again. The waitress brought us our beers and we sat and watched the blonde dance. Her breasts were somewhat like fried eggs. And that gave it a strange effect. All the dancing and bouncing around kept the nipples erect. Erect nipples on fried eggs? The rest of her was more like Minnesota farm girl. Big milky hide without a tan. A band of pale stretch marks around her waist that meant she'd really been fat at one time or she'd had a hell of a large baby. She'd used body powder but in the right light, as she turned this way and that, the pebbled and streaky grain of the skin showed like the texture of a piece of woven cloth.

We were about through with the second beer when the girls changed on the stage. The big blonde, Ellen, got down and the waitress went over to her and said a few words and nodded in our direction. Ellen nodded and slipped a short red poncho over her head and came over to our table.

"You want to talk to me?" I was wrong. It wasn't Minnesota. It was more like south Georgia or northern Florida.

"Sit down and have a drink," I said.

"Thanks." Hump got a chair from a nearby table and she sat between us with her back to the stage. She turned long enough to get the waitress' attention and made a drinking motion with her cupped hand. "She also said you had some money for me."

I got out a five and put it on the table next to my beer can. She reached for it but I put a palm on it and covered it. "I want to get in touch with Peggy Holt."

"Cop?"

"Friends of her family back in North Carolina. They haven't heard from her in a long time. They knew I was here in town and they asked me to look her up. The only thing is the address they gave me isn't good anymore."

"How'd you get to me?"

"Dumb luck. Somebody said she worked as a waitress here for a time."

Ellen turned and nodded in the direction of the office. "Martin could have told you."

"He said he couldn't care less," I said.

"That's his version of it," Ellen said. "He's had her followed for the last few weeks."

"Jealous?"

"Yes." A new thought seemed to strike her. "Now, take you ..."

"Not me," I said. "I'm a bit too old to be one of her jealous lovers."

"I don't know about that." Her eyes still appraised me. "I don't think Peggy ever thought about how old a man was." Without turning her body she eased her head around and faced Hump. "You must be the strong and silent type."

"I talk when the business is over." Hump gave her a grin that told her he'd eat her up and chew on the bones if he wanted to.

"How do you know Martin was having Peggy followed?"

"She told me," Ellen said.

"When?"

"A few days ago ... the last time I saw her."

"Where was that?"

"I ran into her at the Colonial store, the one down near the corner of Eleventh street. We got to the check-out counter at the same time. On the way out she said Martin was still bothering her. I told her I thought that was silly. So she said she'd show me. She offered me a ride home and as we were going out of the parking lot she went out of her way to pass a blue 1970 Impala. She said the man in the car had been following her for almost two weeks. And she was sure that Martin had hired him to do it."

"You get a look at him?"

"He saw us and turned his face away. I couldn't tell how tall he was but he had reddish hair cut in a flat-top and a narrow face."

"He follow you?"

She nodded. "He stayed about a block back, but it was him all right."

"How was Peggy taking this ... being tailed?"

"She tried to make jokes about it, but I could tell she was afraid. You know how some men are. They just hang on and hang on, even after it's over. Martin's that way." It was getting to be a pattern with her, talking to me and then turning to Hump. I think Hump's silence bothered her. "I bet you throw away more than you keep," she said to him.

"I keep the quiet ones," Hump said.

"Look," Ellen said, "I don't want to do anything to hurt Peggy. She doesn't make friends easily and I don't think she has many.

I don't even know if she considers me a friend. But whatever we are, I don't think I can stab her in the back for five dollars."

"That's melodrama," I said. "Nobody's asking you to stab anybody in the back. The five's for your time."

"And even if I don't tell you where Peggy is, the five's mine?"

"Sure." It might be a con but I'd been conning her up to now and maybe turnabout is fair play. I pushed the five over to her and Hump and I watched while she creased the bill and lifted her poncho. She stuffed the five into her swim suit bottom. I got a flash of pubic hair. Maybe that was supposed to be worth the five. I didn't think so, but I guess most of the men who came into Eve's Place would.

"And you're not going to ask me again?"

"If you're going to tell me I guess you'll do it. If not…" I shrugged. "You wouldn't want us to twist your arm, would you?"

"You do that kind of thing?"

"Not as a rule," I said.

"Not to pretty girls," Hump said.

"All right then." Ellen scooped up her drink and pushed back her chair. "It's been good meeting you."

If we hadn't been so close to getting the information I think I'd have laughed. There she was prancing away with my five and Hump was about to break up over it. He liked to see me beaten by a con that I'd started myself. Hump leaned over the table toward me. "Hot damn, that girl just faked you out of your underwear."

And then, as if it had been a game the whole time, Ellen whirled around and came back to our table. She leaned toward me and said, "You know the High Museum down between Fifteenth and Sixteenth?"

I said I did.

"On Fifteenth street, facing the side of the Museum, there's a large yellow house with a lot of stairs going up to the front door."

"Five or six houses from the corner?"

"That's it. She lives behind the yellow house, in a garage apartment."

I nodded. "Thanks, Ellen."

But she was through with me. Her attention was on Hump. "You come back by yourself sometime."

"I'll do it," Hump said. From the sour look that passed over his face as soon as her back was turned I wouldn't book bets that he would. Not in twenty years.

The driveway beside the yellow house was steep and narrow and Hump passed it up and parked along the curb out front. We followed the driveway and passed the side of the house. There the driveway curved and led us to the garage. There was room for two cars but both spaces were empty. At the rear right corner of the garage there was an old gas floor furnace and as we passed it cut in with a whomp-whomp.

The stairs were around on the left side. I stopped at the foot of the stairs.

"You sure you want to go up there?" Hump asked. "Might scare her away?"

"Don't like it myself," I said, "but I've got to be sure Ellen didn't send us out to hunt snipe while she called Peggy and warned her about us."

We clomped up the stairs. On the landing we stopped and I could hear the faint sound of rock music coming from inside. I didn't see a door bell so I rapped on the door frame. I waited a minute and tried again. Still no sound from inside but the faint rock music. I pulled the screen door open and tried the door. It came open and I pushed it the rest of the way.

"Watch the road," I said over my shoulder to Hump.

I went inside. I was in a narrow living room, at least I thought that was what it was. Flush against the wall to my right was a waterbed with a spread over it. The transistor radio was on the waterbed. The battery was low but it was still trying. Facing the waterbed were a couple of bean-bag chairs. Between the chairs and the waterbed was a low coffee table.

The bedroom was straight ahead. The door was open and there didn't seem to be anyone in there. To my left there was a partly open door. I went in that direction. From what I could see through the partly open door it was a kitchen-dining room combination. I reached the doorway and swung the door open the rest of the way.

Even as I pushed the door I could see the drops of blood on the floor. That prepared me and I wasn't surprised when I saw the man face down at the kitchen table. There was an overturned cereal bowl on the floor next to the table. The man was face down in a mess of cornflakes and milk. Careful to avoid the blood I moved closer and looked at him. He wasn't anybody I knew. At least he wasn't from what I could see of the part of his face that wasn't in the soggy cornflakes.

He'd been shot in the back several times. His right hand, pushed out to the side, was clenched, full of cornflakes.

CHAPTER FOUR

O f all the detectives over at the department I had to draw the
one who liked me the least and wanted my hide the most. He
was Bear Hodge and the dislike went back even before I'd left the
force under the cloud. It went back to everything we'd ever been
involved in. Everything from a pick-up game of touch football
on Saturdays in Piedmont Park to playing poker with some of
the guys. If it was football I could always plan on him seeking me
out a few times each afternoon with an elbow or a knee. If it was
poker I knew that he and one of his buddies would try to whip-
saw me when a big hand came along.

The name fitted him. He looked like one of those friendly
cartoon bears. The same dumb look too. That was misleading
because, if anything, he was animal sly. Nothing much got past
him. And under what looked like summer bear fat he was hard
and mean and tough. He'd been a college wrestler before the
World War II, and there was a story about him that right after
Japan surrendered he'd been stationed in Tokyo and he'd taken
up judo just for the hell of it. He'd passed his black belt exami-
nation by humiliating one of the hometown Japanese boys in
a match and he'd done it with such contempt that he'd almost
caused a riot and a new outbreak of the war.

Now I was the one on the mat with him. He gave Hump one
look and motioned him over to the bean-bag chair that was fur-
thest away from us. "You know who that is in there?"

"No," I said.

"His name is trouble and your ass is on the wood stove," Bear said.

"I didn't kill him and I don't know him. How am I in trouble?"

"His name is Randy King. The name King mean anything to you?"

I shook my head.

"Maybe Ben King means something to you?"

It did. He was the last legitimate hero the force had. He was the kind of cop who lived his life like he thought there was some kind of shield around him, like he believed he had a charmed life. In the end it turned out he didn't. Not that he got killed. Nothing like that. He hadn't been killed when maybe he should have. He'd gone after two men who'd been surprised in the act of robbing a motel. They'd been holed up in the motel with the night clerk as a hostage when Ben King made his try. He got the night clerk out safely and he killed one of the small timers and wounded the other. But a slug damaged his spine and he was off the force now and crippled pretty badly. The word was that he could still get around some. He'd never been one of my favorites. I didn't like showy cops.

He and Bear, I remembered, were pretty close, like brothers.

"His brother?" I asked.

Bear grinned at me, a wicked grin, like a teacher encouraging a slow learner. "His kid brother. His favorite and only brother."

That broke it. I glanced over at Hump and shook my head. Without an invitation from Bear I went over to the other bean-bag chair and sat down. It didn't happen often but my legs didn't seem to want to hold me up anymore.

Bear followed me and leaned over me. "All right, now," he said, "tell me that horseshit story again." He shook out a cigarette and wet the end and rolled it into the corner of his mouth. "I think it started with you looking for a girl named Peggy Holt whose real name is Margaret Simpson."

I told the story three more times. Then Hump told his version of it and I was in the middle of re-telling it a fourth time when I heard the slow clomp-clomp coming up the outside stairs toward the landing. Bear heard it too and he broke off in the process of needling me and rushed to the outside door.

From where I was sitting I'd been watching the crew work their way slowly through everything in the bedroom and in the bathroom beyond. The police photographer had finished with the body of Randy King in the kitchen and, although the meat wagon was outside and the stretcher was in the kitchen, they'd made no move to take the body away. As soon as I heard the clomp-clomp I knew why. They'd been waiting for Ben King and now he'd arrived. I guess if finding the body of Ben King's brother got me in trouble I was about nose deep in it.

"Ben, come in," Bear said at the door. He pushed the screen door away and flattened himself against the door frame to make room for Ben to pass. I hadn't seen Ben since before the shootout. Still, I guess I should have known how he'd look. The huge shape that staggered through the doorway wasn't the Ben King I remembered. The arms and the shoulders were the same, but the rest of him wasn't. His body had gone soft and bloated and he looked like a rubber casing filled with liquid. There was agony and sweat on his face as he moved, legs half dangling, half dragging. His hair'd been black the last time I saw him. Now it was gray and shaggy. I'd never liked Ben or his grandstand cop work, but it hurt a little watching him. Bear wasn't quite sure what to do. He wanted to help but Ben wasn't having any of that. He got through the doorway alone. Once he was inside he took his eyes off the floor long enough to look at me briefly.

"Where's Randy?"

Bear pointed toward the kitchen door. Ben made a slow turn on his metal crutches and headed that way. Bear jumped in front of him and swung the door open. The two attendants who'd come with the meat wagon were in there, lounging around the kitchen counter and smoking. One look at Ben King and they scurried out of the room. Bear slammed the door closed behind them.

The two attendants stood around the living room looking at us while we looked at them. They didn't have anything to say and neither did we. It seemed a long time, that silence in the kitchen, but it wasn't more than two or three minutes at the most. Bear came out first and held the door open for Ben. On his way past the two attendants Bear nodded and they went into the kitchen and eased the door closed behind them.

Ben made his slow and painful way toward us. Before he reached us Bear went into the bedroom and came back with a chair. He placed it opposite me, just a few feet from where I sat. Ben eased down into the chair and just looked at me. He gave a long throaty sigh and I could see that his hands were sweaty and red from the strain of dragging himself around. He waited until his breathing was even and then he said, "All right, Hardman, tell me about this."

"I've told it to Bear God knows how many times," I said.

"Tell it again," Ben said.

"You're not a cop anymore, either. I'm going to tell it one more time but that'll be when they're taking it down. You want to know my story, you ask Bear."

Ben's hand jerked on one of the metal crutches and I thought, for just a second, that I was going to get the bottom end of it across my face. I don't know what stopped him. In the old days nothing in the world would have stopped Ben from putting a fist against the side of my head. Maybe the time on his back and the pain had taught him patience.

The hand relaxed on the crutch and he turned to Bear. "How do you see it?"

"From the blood I'd say he was shot as he stood in the doorway, probably from the living room. I'd say small caliber slugs, maybe something like a lady's gun. Might be a .22. He probably fell down, got up and staggered over to the table. Made it to the chair and that was all."

"No phone in the kitchen?" Ben said.

"In the bedroom," Bear said.

"I wonder he didn't try to make it to the phone."

"He might of known he couldn't make it," Bear said. "It happens like that."

Slowly, painfully, Ben King's head turned toward me. "This girl you were looking for ... Ben said her name was Peggy Holt."

I nodded.

"Dark-haired, long hair, a sort of older hippie girl?"

"That's the one," I said.

"Who're you working for?"

"You know I'm not a private investigator." I said. "A lawyer named Jack Smathers asked me to do him a favor. I do favors for friends." It was the question that had to be asked. It was the one I'd have asked first. Bear was walking around it, like it had never occurred to him. There wasn't any reason for me to tiptoe past it. "You got any idea why Randy was here, Ben?"

It hurt him to say it. I could see that in his face and the way his lips trembled. "The stupid kid, he was living with her. Moved out on his wife, Betty, and his boy. I did everything I could to break them up, but he wouldn't listen to me. And now this happens."

I think he would have broken it off at this point if he could have. He didn't like saying all this in front of me and in front of Hump. But it had to be said and it was too much pain and trouble to return to the kitchen and tell it to Bear in there.

He wasn't sure but he thought that Randy had met Peggy about two years before. That was when there'd been a storefront police station down on the Strip between Eighth and Tenth. At the time there were rumors that some of the hippie chicks were making themselves available to the cops. They called it "screwing the pigs toward friendly." Maybe that was how Peggy and Randy had met. It must have been casual at the time. Most of those affairs down there at the time had been. In time there was so much of the mixing between the cops and the young hippie chicks that it probably brought about the closing of the storefront station. Many of the wives of the cops working the area began to complain that their husbands were bringing home cases of clap. That hadn't happened with Randy. He'd remained on foot patrol down there and he'd done good work. Several good arrests on his record. But two months ago he'd started staying away some nights, as many as two or three nights a week. His wife, Betty, had called Ben and he had gone down to the Strip and talked with some of the men who worked with Randy. That was when the girl came up. It looked like the affair had bloomed again. Ben knew it wasn't any good trying to reason with Randy, so he'd used his influence to have him transferred off the Strip. He was sent back downtown to a desk job in the records and evidence storeroom. It hadn't helped much and a week ago Randy'd moved out on Betty. The word down on the Strip was that he'd moved in with the tramp and set up house. Ben had seen him a time or two over at the department. Randy wouldn't listen to him. He'd said Ben was talking old, out of date, morality. He, Randy, was going to do damned well what he wanted to and if Ben didn't like that he could look the other way and walk on the other side of the street. Ben had made one more try. He'd called at the department and tried to reach Randy. He was told that Randy had taken two weeks of leave and they didn't know how to get in touch with him.

"If I could have seen him maybe this wouldn't have happened," Ben said.

Bear nodded along with him. "Well, you did all you could, Ben."

"It wasn't enough."

"It was all you or anybody else could have done," Bear said.

Ben gave a slow jerk of his head which meant that he accepted it the way Bear meant it. But it didn't satisfy him. Now he was done with his telling and it was my turn. "Hardman, we never got along."

"That's true. I never liked you and you never liked me."

The bellow, when it came, shouldn't have stunned me the way it did. The quiet way just wasn't Ben's style. "But goddam it, Hardman, that's my only brother in there dead and if you think that I'm going to let you or anybody else cover up or hide. ...."

"I've told it straight. I don't have anybody to protect. Call Jack Smathers at his office. Go by Eve's Place and talk to a blonde named Ellen. Call Edward Simpson in Chapel Hill. Do all this or any part of it you want to, but stop yelling at me."

It got thick and still. Even the noise in the other room where the search crew was working stopped for a time. I braced myself. I saw it two ways. Ben would swing the crutch at me or Bear would do his heavy work for him. I was about to place my bet on Bear when Ben relaxed and shook his head slowly, again and again.

"I guess that's fair. I wouldn't be yelling if it wasn't my brother in there."

I shook my head. That wasn't true but I didn't think it was worth arguing about. "I'm sorry about your brother, Ben. I didn't know him but I think I know how you feel. If I knew who'd killed him I'd be glad to hold him for you while you beat the shit out of him. But I don't and that's all there is to it."

"It must have been the girl," Bear said. He held out a huge hand toward me. "I'll take that picture."

I handed him the snapshot of Peggy Holt. Or Simpson or whatever.

"Is that her? Let me see it." Ben took the picture and stared down at it for a long time. "So that's what she looks like."

"I understand her hair's longer now."

A young cop, one of the two I'd seen working through the bedroom and the bathroom, came into the living room carrying a small cardboard box.

"Found this in the back of the closet. I thought you'd want to see it." He emptied the box onto the low coffee table. It was a bundle that looked like a plastic tablecloth. He unrolled it and spread out the articles that had been inside. A bundle of glassine bags, a box of powdered milk and a container of strychnine.

"Dope," Bear said, "somebody's been cutting and packaging that crap here."

"Why the strychnine?" Ben asked.

"Something they do sometimes. The stuff gets cut too much and the user doesn't get the jolt he expects. The strychnine puts the jolt in. It's kind of a booster."

That was the part I'd left out. The visit to the Wildwood Connector and the story he'd heard about Peggy Holt doing some dealing in hard stuff now.

"That's it," Ben said. "Randy must have found out what she was doing, that she was dealing in drugs, and she killed him to keep it quiet. Damn her to hell."

That was a bit too simple for me. It skirted around too much. I let it pass. It was easier for him that way.

After a time, Bear let us go. It was tied up neatly and had a ribbon on it and he didn't need us anymore.

CHAPTER FIVE

I caught the secretary between a whereas and a therefore and while she tried to remember where she'd seen me before I said, "He might be expecting me" and rammed the inner office door open. The door hit a bookcase of law reference works with a good thunk and Jack lost his place in the volume of *Georgia Appeals* that he had braced on his knee.

"Do I get free legal services when I work for you?"

"What? Look, Jim, I don't …"

"Bear hasn't called you yet?"

"No. Why would …"

"You'll get your call or maybe a personal visit," I said. "It seems you sent me out to find a body."

It stunned him and I got a look inside him. The barbed hooks, flesh grown over them until they're almost forgotten, working their way out of the protective pockets. I'd seen a man have a heart attack one afternoon on Broad street and he'd looked like Jack the moment he'd made the grab for the lamp post.

"Not her," I said. "Not the golden crotch."

Jack kept a bottle of cheap scotch in the bottom desk drawer. He got it out and we had a taste right from the bottle. It was so raw it made me regret, right away, even the token courtesy drink. It went down smoother with Jack. He passed the bottle back toward me and I shook my head. "But I'll take an ounce or so of it home with me to remove a couple of corns on my little toes."

"It's not for me," Jack said. "I keep it around for divorce settlement conferences. When the husband finds out what it's going to cost him to get rid of his wife he usually needs a bracer." He took a deep breath and let it out slowly. I'd given him the fifty words or less rundown on what Hump and I had found at the garage apartment on Fifteenth. Now he was calm enough to put his lawyer's mind to picking at it.

"Then they're looking for Peggy?"

"Unless somebody walked in and confessed in the last twenty minutes or so. You've got to admit it looks strange. Randy killed in his breakfast and no sign of her anywhere."

"Or of the child, Maryann," he said.

"That too," I said.

The door to the outer office opened and Hump walked in. "Had trouble finding a parking spot" he said. "How's our lawyer doing?"

"Recovering," I said. I pushed it back at Jack: "Now we know two people who didn't kill Randy King. I didn't and Hump didn't. That leaves about a million and a half who could have. That includes residents and visitors."

"Jack here's a resident," Hump said.

"That's true enough," I said. "I hope you can account for all the time since I left your office this morning."

"Up to maybe an hour and a half ago," Hump said.

"I'd put it closer to two hours at the latest," I said. The wall clock over one of the book cases put the time at ten of five. "Say, three o'clock at the outer edge."

"That's late to be having breakfast," Jack said.

"I looked around the kitchen before the police came. Wasn't much choice. I think even the mice were hungry there. Trash was full of take-out boxes and chicken bones."

"Too busy screwing and cutting and bagging dope," Hump said.

Jack flushed a bit and held himself down. "I can account for the whole afternoon, except for five minutes here and there." He spread his hand in a hopeless gesture. "All right, that girl tore me up. Right down to the bone marrow. But I wouldn't kill over her. If I'd killed anyone it would be her, not some short-time lover of hers."

"That leaves at least one out-of-towner," I said.

"I guess we'd better touch the bases," Jack said. He pushed down the intercom lever and told the secretary to put in a call to Edward Simpson in Chapel Hill. He flipped the lever back to "closed" and said, "Simpson was with me from 9 A.M. until he left us here at the office.

"That would be 11:15 or 11:20," I said.

"Could it have happened before 11:15?" Jack asked.

"Not likely," I said.

"Any way of finding out what the police thinking is?"

"I can put in a call to Art Maloney when he comes on his shift," I said. "He probably won't be there for another hour or two."

The intercom sputtered. "Your call to Chapel Hill, Mr. Smathers."

Jack picked up the phone. "I'd like to speak to Edward Simpson, please. This is Jack Smathers in Atlanta." He listened and pulled a pad toward him. "Did he say what flight that was?" He made a note on the pad. "And what time it'll arrive?" He wrote that down below the flight number and turned the pad so that I could read it. The flight number didn't mean anything. The time did: 5:42. That meant he was probably just leaving Atlanta while we were making the call up there. Even though the ride out to Hartsfield took some time, there was still a matter of about four hours that Simpson would have to account for. And they were in the red area, the time when the killing had probably taken place. Say he was lying to us and knew where his ex-wife was. He'd have all the time in the world to beat us there. It had taken us time to work our way to the garage apartment. The lunch at the Fisherman's Inn, the visit to the Wildwood Connector, the blonde at Eve's Place.

The blonde at Eve's Place. That stopped me. It hadn't meant much to me then and now it did. The man in the Impala, the one with red hair that had been following Peggy Holt around for a couple of weeks. If he was still tailing her around he might know some of the answers the cops wanted. And he might know where Peggy Holt was now.

Jack was winding up his conversation. I made my guess that the person on the other end of the line was probably Simpson's second wife. "Have Edward call me as soon as he arrives. Either here at the office or at my home phone. I think he has both of the numbers." He made his goodbye and put the phone back on its cradle.

I got up and nodded toward Hump. "I just had a thought, Jack. If we're still working I'd like to follow through on it."

"Might as well," he said.

As we were heading out the door I heard him call the blonde secretary in to take a few notes. More than likely, I thought, a rundown of how he's spent the late morning and the afternoon.

"A red-haired guy in a 1970 Impala. You got any idea how we run him to ground?"

"You're the ex-cop," Hump said. "I always depend on you in situations like this."

We'd picked up Hump's car at a lot down the street and we were fighting our way into the late afternoon traffic. It was hell this time of day. Peachtree Street seemed like a narrow bottle-neck that all the traffic had to work its way through. I guess it was our day in the barrel and we could look forward to about a thirty-minute stop and start the drive back down to the Strip.

"We could always ask Martin," Hump said.

"And, of course, he'd be happy to tell us."

"If we asked him the right way."

"I ever talk to you about leaping over gaps?" I asked.

"Not while I was sober enough to remember."

"It goes like this. We know a red-haired guy in a 1970 Impala was following Peggy Holt. We know that for sure because the blonde, Ellen, saw him. Then comes the gap. Peggy's just pissed off Martin so she figures that he's the one pasted the tail on her. That's natural enough. And she tells Ellen and she believes it because it seems natural enough to her also. And then Ellen tells us. ..."

"Who else?"

"That girl's been busy. Pissing off dudes and now up to her ass in dope. Could be Raymond who put the tail on her. Could be Federal. Could be State narcs. And any one of the old boyfriends."

"Sounds strange to me," Hump said. "You notice something? They start out hard. Like they'd like to stuff a broken beer bottle up her and then it changes and they act like it wasn't really so bad."

"I noticed."

"Like to meet that girl myself," Hump said.

"Think on the red-haired guy then."

"I am. I am."

It didn't make sense going around in circles so we decided to have a beer. Hump parked on the old part of Ninth ... Peachtree Place, where it didn't cross Peachtree and we walked down toward Eighth and into the Stein Club.

At one time the Stein Club had been a favorite watering place down in that part of town. The customers ran from professional people in their twenties and thirties to a select group of interesting alcoholics. It had been a place where the talk could be interesting on a good day and only mildly dull on a bad day.

Back in July of 1972 the 18-year-old vote-and-drink laws went into effect and the Stein changed. Some of the old regulars moved on to other places. Some of the old customers still came in, refusing to give it up as lost. It was a kind of silent war between the street kids and the middle class. And I had a feeling that the street people would win. They understood hassle better than the up and coming middle class did and they'd learned to endure it better.

Hump got a pitcher and glasses while I dug out a dime and went over to the single pay phone. A long haired girl who wasn't wearing much underwear was on the phone. From what I overheard she was talking to her mother. She kept saying things like "You don't even try to understand me" and every now and then she'd whine, "Oh, mother..." It was a good act. She really sounded unhappy. From the way she was eyeing a street guy back at the big round table I was pretty sure she was just staging an argument with her mother so she could stay out all night if she got an offer. Finally, just when I'd about decided to come back later, she said, "Well, if that's the way you feel about it..." and hung up.

I leaned in after her and put in my dime. I dialed Art Maloney's home number. He answered on about the sixth ring and that meant he was probably dripping shower water all over the bedroom. "Art? Jim here."

"Yeah?"

"Found a body today. Randy King's body."

"I heard," he said. "Bear woke me up to ask what I thought of you."

"And you said?"

"I told him you weren't dumb enough to commit a murder and then stand around and try to play word games with the police."

"Is that all you told them?"

"Not really," Art said. "I told them you lied sometimes to save your own neck, but if your neck wasn't involved he could believe you."

"Did Bear seem to buy that?"

"I think so." He barked a dry, harsh cough into the phone. "You call me for any special reason?"

I told him about the tail we thought had been on Peggy Holt.

"Bear's not going to like this. He's going to think you were holding out on him."

I ignored the warning in that. "On the chance he might be a P.I. maybe you could get a make on him over at licensing. Somebody there might know a P.I. who fits the description."

He said he'd check it out and call me back. I gave him the number of the Stein.

He called back twenty minutes later. "Too easy," he said. "There's a guy named Harry Harper, seems to specialize in divorce work and skip-tracing. Has an office in the old Fraser Building on Mitchell. Just to be sure it was the right one I had it checked in Motor Vehicles. He does own a 1970 Impala."

"Thanks, Art."

"Don't just thank me," he said. "Let me know if it leads you anywhere."

Before going back to the table I got the city phone directory and the yellow pages from behind the counter. I gave Hump the white pages and told him to see if he could find a Harry Harper listed. I looked in the yellow pages under Investigators. He hadn't taken one of the block ads. He'd settled for a single line listing.

"He got a middle initial?" Hump asked.

I looked at the single line listing. "An R," I said.

"Apartment 2D, Kingsbridge Apartments on Peachtree Road."

"You know where that is?"

"Not exactly," Hump said.

I returned the books to the bar. When I was back at the table across from Hump I asked him if he'd ever met a P.I.

"Not to speak to," he said. "But I think one was following me around one time when I was doing this married woman. At least, when the divorce trial was going on he testified he'd followed me and the girl around some nights and he'd seen us go into my apartment and right after that the lights went off."

"You didn't see him?"

"I'm not even sure the dude was around at all. The shit that makes me wonder is that stuff about the lights going off. You see, that girl and I had a thing about doing it with the lights on and watching it happen." He drained the last of his beer and grinned at me. "Of course, I didn't think it would do any good to get up there and say the dude was lying, that we only did it with the lights on. Somebody might have misunderstood that."

It was after six and getting dark. We got on West Peachtree and headed back downtown. I had some doubts that Harper would still be in his office. Unless he kept night hours. Still, if he didn't want to be found, we might be hunting for a day or two. I decided we might as well locate the office in case we might have to stake it out later.

Mitchell is a mixed street. To the east it runs toward the State offices and the State Capitol. To the west, starting about at Pryor, it turns bad. It seems to exist just for the day labor places and the bars are open at sunrise. There are some old established businesses in the west part of Mitchell but they look like they'll be moving as soon as they get over being stunned by the changes that are going on in the neighborhood.

It was the west part of Mitchell that we were heading for. We parked in a lot near Forsyth and Mitchell and walked west. We'd gone about a block or so, searching the building fronts as we went, and I'd gone a bit ahead when Hump called me back. "This is it, I think," he said. The light was bad but we could make the first part of the lettering in the concrete, FRAS...The rest was chipped away or pollution had been eating it.

Harper Investigations was listed in Room 318 on the lobby directory. There wasn't an elevator. We found the stairwell and started our climb up. The smell of crap and urine was strong there. More than likely some winos slept there on cold nights and they couldn't find the bathroom or didn't go to the trouble to look for it. I was holding my breath by the time we reached the second floor landing. I was snorting like a boxer the last flight up and even when we pushed through the third floor door and found the hallway it wasn't much better.

We found Room 318 at the far end of the hall. There wasn't a light showing. Just to be sure I knocked on the frosted glass and when there wasn't an answer I tried the door. It was locked. I found a note pad tacked to the door right under the frosted glass. I considered that for a moment and had about decided against it when Hump said, "Might be worth a lie or two." I wrote down my name and phone number and added a brief message that I had a job for him. If we found him the lie wouldn't matter. If we continued to miss him he might very well call me and set up a meeting. The chance to make a few dollars might draw him out. If his office was any indication I was fairly certain he needed it.

On the way back down the stairs we passed two winos on the stairs between the second floor landing and the lobby. They were hunched over, shivering, passing a fifth of Thunderbird back and forth.

It was getting toward my suppertime. I could feel the gnawing and the first growls were beginning, but we got Hump's car and drove back out West Peachtree—out past where it changed into Peachtree Road and kept going. After we passed Piedmont Hospital, Hump said he needed gas and I paid for it and listed the seven dollars on an expense page in my notebook. So far the expenses hadn't run too high for the day. Twenty-five for the Wildwood Connector, five for Ellen at Eve's Place and the gas money. All that considered, I decided if the hunt went on much longer Hump and I might as well have supper on Simpson's wife's money.

The Kingsbridge Apartments looked like a forward-thinking management had decided to change its name rather than spend the money for the renovations it needed. Just a guess. It certainly sounded like a fancier address than it really was.

From the road we could see the three flat, long, train like buildings. They were made of red brick and seemed to have eight or ten apartments in each building. A postage stamp private yard went with each and there were shallow porches with some aluminum tube furniture. It didn't, as far as I could see, have a swimming pool. The parking was in back. Hump followed the pitted paved road and parked. From the back it didn't look much better, unless you liked garbage cans and a few rusting charcoal grills. Hump got out and waited, holding the door open while I got out my notebook again and checked the apartment number by the inside light. "2D," I said.

The lighting was dim between the first two buildings. Most of the light came from a porch lamp at the far end, away from us. Hump stopped and turned off the walk. He squinted at a number over the door and came back. "4D," he said. We back-tracked two porches. Hump reached the porch before I did and flicked on his lighter to read the number. It was the right one. He put an eye against the glass part of the door and peered in for a few seconds. "No lights."

I reached around him and tried the door bell. I could hear it ringing inside. Almost immediately the porch light went on next door, in front of apartment 1D. The screen door swung open and a little withered bird of a woman stormed out onto the porch. Her hair was up in curlers and she was wearing a red bathrobe that she clutched at the throat. I put her age at fifty or so, the time when it hits women that the American dream is over and the nasty creeps in.

"It's about time you showed up," she shrieked at us. "You know when I called the first time? Four o'clock, that's when. No wonder the criminals are taking over the city."

I stared into the glare from the porch light.

"First thing in the morning I'm going to call the Mayor's office. I pay my taxes and I think the police …"

Hump stepped into it before I'd decided how to play it. "What seems to be the problem, ma'am?"

"That poor little girl … I think Mr. Harper kidnapped that poor child. She cried the whole time she was in the apartment, like her heart was breaking."

"Did you see the little girl?" I asked. "How old-would you say she was?"

"Seven, I think. Kind of skinny with black hair."

"What makes you think she was kidnapped?"

"The walls are so thin you can hear everything that happens next door. The poor thing kept saying she wanted her mama and Mr. Harper kept telling her to shut up."

"There wasn't anybody else with them?"

"Just Mr. Harper and the girl."

"When did they leave?" Hump asked.

"About five o'clock." Anger spurted out at us again. "That was when I called you the second time."

I squared my shoulders and gave Hump my best professional manner. "I think we'd better look into this." I opened the screen door and tried the knob. Locked. I put a shoulder to the door and tried to spring the lock. It didn't give. "We might have to kick it in," I said to Hump.

"No need to do that," the woman said. "He leaves a spare key in his mail box."

"That'll save a door." Hump reached own into the mail box and brought out the key. While he unlocked the door I turned to the woman. "It might not seem like it," I said, "but we do appreciate you calling us." I got out my notebook and pen. "Would you give us your name, please?"

"Mrs. Carrie Newmark." she said.

I wrote that down. "It isn't every citizen who'd go to the trouble."

"If I ever do again I ought to have my head examined," she said. She backed toward the door and went inside and slammed the door shut behind her. The porch light snapped off.

I didn't know how much time we had. There was always the chance that the cops had put off answering her calls. Sooner or later they'd probably send a cruiser out to calm her down. They'd probably marked her down as a pest call, but even those got answered in time.

I found the switch to the overhead light. It was a neat living room. The rug looked like it had been cleaned in the last day or two and the furniture had been dusted. There was a large bookcase to the left, directly facing the sofa and I went over there and squatted down to read some titles. Except for a few paperbacks of the best seller type, the books were all concerned with law. There were several volumes of the *Encyclopedia of Georgia Law* and perhaps half of a set of *Georgia Code Annotated*. The other law books seemed to be texts. I opened one of them and found Harper's name inside along with the seal of John Marshall University, a small law school in downtown Atlanta. I don't know how well accredited John Marshall is but I assume some of the graduates pass the Georgia Bar exam now and then.

There was an envelope in the book which was being used as a marker. I shook it out of the envelope and read it. It had the John Marshall letterhead and it was a short note to Harper saying that he could resume his study of law as soon as he'd paid his back tuition which totaled $248.24. The letter was dated about three years before.

Hump had left the living room to me. He'd gone into the back part of the apartment. "In here, Jim."

There was a narrow hallway and beyond that to the left a kitchen and to the right a bedroom. Hump was in the kitchen. He pointed down into the sink. A cup that showed the dregs of hot chocolate and a glass that had some water in it and the smell of bourbon.

"Nice guy," Hump said. "Gives his kidnap victims a cup of hot chocolate."

"If it's kidnapping," I said.

"What else?"

"You're guessing the little girl is Peggy Holt's kid?"

"That's my guess," Hump said, "and it's probably yours too."

"World's full of six or seven year old girls with black hair. For all we know the kid could be Harper's daughter."

"No sign a kid lives here," he said.

I shook my head at him. It was a lot of talk and it wasn't getting us anywhere. I left him in the kitchen and crossed the hallway to the bedroom. All that gap-leaping bothered me. There wasn't any real proof the little girl had been Maryann Simpson. As far as we knew the child was still with her mother. On the other hand, Peggy Holt had a history of dumping Maryann when the heat was on, and with Randy King dead back at her apartment, the heat was certainly on and more. What bothered me was the question of how Peggy Holt could go from being the "tailed" person to someone who could turn the child over to her shadow. If that was what had happened.

I switched on the overhead light. It was a small bedroom. A queen-sized bed with a headboard of some kind of bleached oak. A matching chest of drawers with two of the four drawers pulled far out and hanging. Beyond the bed a closet with the door open.

On the bed with the raised top toward me, an old battered leather suitcase. I moved around the bed and looked down into it. Harper had been packing for a trip. It was neat and careful packing. A half a dozen shirts, about the same number or boxer shorts and t-shirts, some ankle length socks, a neat stack of laundered handkerchiefs. And in one corner a soap-stained and water-discolored dopp kit.

Hump came in and looked over my shoulder. "Was that dude leaving town?"

Hump pointed at the pulled-out drawers. "He's neat."

"Was and must have changed his mind," I said.

Hump pointed at the pulled-out drawers. "You notice the rest of the place? Everything in its place. Cup and glass in the sink. Ash trays empty and wiped out."

"Means he left in a hurry," I said.

"Something changed on him. He had a phone call or somebody was at the front door."

"Or he heard the old lady next door calling the police," I said.

"Something spooked him and he turned into a ghost," Hump said.

Mrs. Newmark put on the porch light first and peered out at us from behind a lace curtain. She said, "Just a minute" and she began unlocking several locks and night latches. She left one chain still on and talked to us through the narrow opening.

"You said Harper left around five. Did he leave by himself?"

"He took the little girl with him."

"No, I mean did he leave with some other people?"

"No, well, not exactly. You see, two men came to his door and rang his doorbell. He was still inside but he didn't answer the door. I thought they were the police I'd called so I went out and asked if they were. One of them laughed at me and the other one said something nasty to me. Something I can't repeat. That was how I knew they weren't police and I went back in the house and locked the door good."

"Harper didn't answer the door?"

"They kept knocking and knocking and ringing the bell and finally they gave up and left."

"And right after that Harper and the little girl left?"

She nodded. "Not ten minutes later. They went out the back door.

"The two men ... what did they look like?"

She squinted at me. "One was about your size but a lot younger. The other one was smaller, maybe about up to your shoulder."

I thanked her and backed away.

"You think there really was a kidnapping?"

"There might be," I said. "We'll put an all points out on him and when we find him we'll see if he can explain this to us."

That seemed to satisfy her and she said goodnight and closed the door. The jangle of chains and the snick of locks followed us part of the way out to the parking lot.

CHAPTER SIX

Art came into the Mandarin and looked around for us in the bar before he came back into the restaurant and found us. He was still wearing the shiny-seated blue suit he'd been wearing for the last seven or eight years. He saw us and nodded and worked his way through the aisle toward our table. He dropped into a seat across the table from me and gave Hump a meager grin. Art's my age and his big round Irish face is beginning to sag a little around the edges. One difference between us is that he works out at the gym and plays handball. I have a feeling he's not going to fall apart quite as soon as I will.

"You eaten yet?" I asked.

"Who the hell eats supper this late in the South?"

"A drink then?"

"All right."

I waved at the waiter and Art ordered a Bud.

"What's all this hurry-up about anyway?" Art asked.

"The P.I. I had you check on. No proof, but I think he's holding Peggy Holt's little girl."

"With or without the mother's consent?" Art asked.

"No way of knowing."

"So far we don't have a complaint of a kidnapping."

"How the hell's she going to complain," I asked, "when the cops are looking all over town for her?"

"Her problem," Art said.

"Are you serious?"

The waiter brought the beer and Art poured off part of it and watched it bubble. "All Peggy Holt has to do is walk into the police station and file a complaint."

"I know that would make it easier for you," I said.

"Oh, shit," Art said. "I know as well as you she's not that stupid." He sipped at the beer. "So you want me to run Harper to ground for you?"

"For yourself," I said.

"Not for you at all, huh?"

"Lord knows. In fact, I'll be damned if I know why I haven't packed it in completely and called it off."

"It's the little girl," Hump said.

"The kid's nothing to me," I said.

Hump just gave me that level look of his. If he had another argument he didn't bother to make it.

Art nodded. "I'll see what we can do. Material witness or something like that."

"That ought to do it."

The business part was over. Art relaxed. "How's Marcy?"

"Fine as far as I know." I looked at my watch. "Right now at some seminar over at Georgia State."

"I didn't get my invitation to the wedding yet," Art said.

"The check I gave the printer bounced. He wouldn't let me have them on credit."

"I'll lend it to you," Art said.

"I don't know why all you marrieds want the rest of us to step into the same tub of crap with you."

"Marcy's not going to wait forever."

"She's a grown woman. Her business what she does."

Hump leaned in, a puzzled look on his face. "Something happening I don't know about?"

I shook my head. "Art's trying to pick a fight with me for some reason."

"No reason I know of," Art said, "unless it's the fact I'm getting tired of being your man over at the department."

"I thought you were trying to solve a killing over there?"

"And passing info out the back door to you is going to help?"

"It might," I said.

"It's not a feeling I like."

"Forget it then," I said. "Hump and I'll find Harper and the kid ourselves."

"Sure." Art placed his glass of beer in the center of the table and pushed his chair back. "Stay in touch."

Hump watched him go stiff-backed through the bar and outside. "He's on the rag today."

"There's pressure over there."

"I never saw Art as the type who'd feel it," Hump said.

"You can't tell until it happens. It looks bad. Young cop, brother of big hero cop, killed in apartment of somebody who's dealing in hard dope. Without being there I know the word that's gone down the pipe. Clean it up and clean it up fast. And if possible, make sure Randy King comes out of it with a new coat of whitewash."

I finished my butterfly shrimp and Hump worked through his order of chicken chow mein. After that he drove me over to the Fisherman's Inn where we'd left my car earlier in the day. I told Hump I'd call him in the morning and drove on home. Marcy'd said she'd try to drop by for a drink after the seminar closed down for the night.

The clock on the nightstand, read by the narrow slant of light from the bathroom, showed the time as 11:48. I'd been dozing for half an hour or so. I guess the sound of the shower had awakened me. I folded a pillow behind my head and waited.

"Do you really have to leave?" I asked her a few minutes later when she stopped in the bathroom doorway, backlit, partly in shadow. Her body was still fine but even with a lover's eye I could see the downward tilt of her breasts and I could remember the slow erosion of skin tone.

"I have an early appointment and you don't seem to get up before noon anymore."

"Tomorrow I'm up early," I said.

"That's what you say now." She moved out of the light. At the closet she turned to put the blade in me one more time. "It doesn't sound like a very good job anyway."

That was the bone we'd been kicking back and forth at each other all night, except for the time we'd been making love. It had stopped then, but I'd felt a stiffness in her I hadn't known before. And it had resumed as soon as she'd got her breath back. She couldn't seem to understand why I hadn't taken one of the jobs that I'd been offered in the last couple of months. My first mistake had been telling her about them. The best of them had come through a reference from Art. It was a position as director of the Atlanta office of Safeguard Security, one of those private security systems. The money was good and there were some promised yearly pay advances if I worked out. What held me back were the regular hours, the 8 to 5 kind of crap I'd never liked. The other job had been as head of security for a chain of discount stores in Georgia and Florida. That meant a certain amount of traveling. I'd used that as my excuse for not taking that job. I didn't want to be away from Atlanta that much. The real reason was that I didn't want a regular job if I could get by without one.

"Sometimes I think you're never going to grow up. I think you're Huck Finn and Hump is your Nigger Jim and you're going to spend the rest of your life floating down some kind of mythical Mississippi River."

"I had a deprived childhood. I never read the book."

"It's not too late," Marcy said.

"I'll buy the book tomorrow."

"No, I meant grow up." Marcy'd finished with her underwear. She took the brown tweed skirt from a hanger and stepped into it.

"It looks like we have some kind of war every night before you go home," I said.

"You'd rather we had them at the beginning of the evening and ruin it all?"

"I'd rather we didn't have them at all," I said.

"I think that can be arranged."

Her tone of voice jolted me. "What do you mean by that?"

"I met a man two weeks ago. A new man in the office. My age. Cultured, well-educated. He likes classical music and ballet. He's been asking me to go out with him and so far I've been putting him off."

"He sounds dreamy," I said. "Wonder why some girl hasn't run off with him before now?"

She ignored the sarcasm. "I think I'll get him to ask me again tomorrow and I'll accept."

"You're a grown girl," I said.

"You always say that."

"I try to mean it too."

I don't know exactly what would have happened if we'd gone on. Maybe we'd have torn too much flesh or we'd have said things we couldn't take back. We didn't get to find out because, at that moment, I heard the dull ring of the front doorbell.

"Who's that?"

"I don't know." I got on a pair of trousers and a t-shirt and my slippers. The bell stopped. There had been one ring and that was all. On the way through the living room I tried to guess who it was. Might be Hump, but I didn't think so. Might be Art if he'd found Harper and the kid. Still, most of the time he called before he came by.

I swung the door open. At first, with the porch light off, I thought whoever it was who'd rung the bell had given up and gone away. Then I heard a scratching noise and a shape swung from the shadows into the doorway and fell toward me. On reflex I stepped away. He hit the floor with a relaxed thud. I bent over him and turned him. He had red hair and a narrow face. Harper. There were blood bubbles on his lips but he wasn't dead yet. I leaned closer. His lips moved a couple of times and nothing came out but more blood. I was about to straighten up when he said, "The bitch, the fucking bitch."

I looked down at his hand and saw clutched there the message I'd left on his note pad at his office. I opened his hand and took it out. He or somebody else had written my address below the message with a pencil.

It was quiet out on the street. I could hear a car engine running and I looked out. The Impala was parked at a crazy angle in front of my house, the headlights still on.

Though I knew better, I tried to find a pulse. There wasn't one. His chest was a mass of blood. It was hard to tell how many times he'd been shot or where he'd been shot … in the back or the front.

I went back into the bedroom and told Marcy to stay in the bedroom unless she wanted to see what violent death looked like. I sat on the edge of the bed and called the department number and asked for Art.

CHAPTER SEVEN

While I waited for the first cruiser to arrive I got Harper by the shoulders and pulled him the rest of the way into the living room so that I could close the door. I'd left him there while I'd finished dressing and when I came back out the temperature in the house seemed to have dropped about thirty degrees. Six or eight inches one way or the other wouldn't matter to the investigation. It did matter to my old busted up and broken-backed furnace. I could hear it grumbling down in the basement.

The cruiser lights hit my front window not long after I'd moved the body and closed the door. I put on a jacket and went outside to meet them. They'd pulled up in my driveway behind my car and Marcy's. I told the uniformed cops that the body was inside and that I'd left the car Harper had driven up in exactly as it was. We walked across the chill-brittle grass stubble and down to the road where the Impala was. It was parked with the nose-end against the lawn and the ass-end out in the road. It was a wonder nobody'd clipped it yet. One of the cops opened the door to the driver's side and cut the ignition and turned the lights off. The other one went back to the cruiser and got a road flare that he placed at the rear of the Impala.

I stood behind the cop who'd cut the ignition and watched while he played his flashlight over the inside of the car. The seat back and bottom on the driver's side was dark and blood-soaked. There were also splattering and small pools on the floorboards. He'd bled a lot and the real wonder was that he'd had enough life left in him to make it across my lawn and up the stairs to the porch.

He snapped off the flashlight. "I have it a second?" He handed it to me and I turned it on and ran the light slowly over the back seat. There was an old army blanket balled up in the corner away from us. Closer up, near the center of the backseat, there was a pair of knitted children's gloves. White with a red trim around the wrist.

I returned the flashlight to him and we went into the house to wait for Art to arrive.

"Why you?" Art asked. "Why not a hospital?"

It was almost an hour later. The meat wagon had come and gone. The body and the Impala had been taken away. The cruiser that had been the first to arrive had gone back to its regular patrol. Art and Marcy and I were alone in the house.

"I'll make a guess if you like."

"Make it," Art said.

"Maybe the shooting took place near here. Sometime between the time Hump and I left his office on Mitchell he dropped by there. He got my address out of the phone book. He was in the middle of something dangerous and maybe he wanted to check me out, wanted to see if what I wanted him for was involved or entirely separate. He might have intended to drop in on me. A surprise visit. After he got shot he remembered me and tried to make it here."

"Why you? What could you do for him?"

"Lord knows what he was thinking. I've never been shot five or six times, so I might never understand what happens to your thinking process in that situation."

Marcy called us from the kitchen. The coffee was ready. Before we sat down at the table I got the part of a bottle of Stock from the cabinet and put it in the center of the table along with three glasses. Art pushed his glass away and I poured for Marcy and myself.

"You seem to be very lucky with witnesses," Art said. "Hump to back you at the garage apartment and Marcy this time."

I sipped at the Stock and gave him my go-to-hell grin. "That's true."

"Next time try to have a witness along who's not your drinking buddy or your girlfriend," he said.

"If I have time to arrange it."

"You don't believe me?" Marcy asked.

"I believe you," Art said. "You might be foolish enough to love the bastard but I don't think you'd lie for him."

I'd been watching her face. Because of the argument in the bedroom—the one Harper had been nice enough to interrupt by dying in my living room—I tried to read her face when Art said "love." It didn't tell me anything at all. If it meant anything at all to her she hid it well.

"That's true," Marcy said. "That is, I wouldn't lie for him."

For a moment I thought Art might ask the question I wanted to ask why she'd qualified it that way. The phone rang in the bedroom. If Art asked the question I wasn't there to hear the answer. The call was for Art, one of the detectives over at the department wanting to talk to him. I called him and we passed each other in the living room.

I sat across the table from Marcy and sipped at the Stock. "Hope you have a good time at the ballet."

"If there's one in town," she said.

"Or the Atlanta Symphony," I said.

"If they're in town."

"Or just talking about literature," I said.

"If we've read the same books."

"You could take turns reading to each other in French and German."

"You are an ass," Marcy said.

Art returned from the bedroom. "One new thing. When they got Harper over to the morgue and undressed him they found an $8 bag in his calf-length socks. It looks like fairly pure stuff. Better than the usual street crap."

"Harper a user?"

"No needle marks," Art said.

"When you say pure, how pure?"

"They're not sure. Have to wait on the lab, but Henry thinks it's fifty-fifty or better."

"What's usual on the street?"

"Maybe thirty percent," Art said.

Marcy pushed back her chair. She put her coffee cup in the sink and went into the bedroom without looking at me. I watched her out of the corner of one eye and I noticed that Art looked puzzled.

"When the quality's that high, what does it mean?" I reached across the table and got the remainder of Marcy's Stock. I poured it into my glass.

"Hard to say. One thing it might mean is that the $8 bag came from somebody fairly close to the source. Usually, no matter how high the quality is at the beginning, it passes through a lot of hands. Each time it gets bought it's cut again, more milk or sugar added as filler. When it hits the street for sale it's thirty percent or less."

"All that cutting equipment at Peggy Holt's apartment. That suggest anything to you?"

"Could be," Art said. "It's the kind of unsupported jump I don't like to make. But let's make it anyway, just for the sake of argument."

"Two bits of support for the argument, if you're going to make the one I think you are. The lady next door to Harper's apartment and the knit gloves in the back of the Impala."

"We checked on that lady, whatever her name is. She'd been reporting prowlers, rapes in the parking lot and such the last year or so. All turned out to be nothing. No wonder the cops didn't hurry over there. And the knit gloves. We don't know they belonged to Maryann Simpson."

"I'll check the gloves out," I said.

"Back to the argument. Peggy Holt's got her hands on some high grade heroin. She cuts a small amount of it and starts passing it around to the middle men. She's saying this is the kind of shit I've got for sale. Now somewhere along the way Harper gets his hands on one of the sample bags. Maybe along with the bag he gets himself an idea. He figures on a way of getting himself a chunk of the dope or some part of the cash it'll bring. He snatches the kid. Peggy can have Maryann back for a price. And Peggy's in no position to go running to the cops about the kidnapping. Could be she does the other thing. She gets herself a couple gun handlers and they go out and find Harper and shoot him and take the kid back."

"Let's muddy the water some. Think about the possibility that whoever killed Harper wasn't working for the mother at all. Just somebody who picked up on Harper's idea."

"Who would that be?"

"A copycat," I said. "The word is that some of the old established firms don't like the competition."

"A move in a drug war?"

"Maybe."

I'd been watching the bedroom door. Marcy came out in her heavy coat and with a scarf over her hair. She paused in the kitchen doorway.

"Leaving?"

"Yes." She said goodnight to Art.

"I'll see you to your car," I said.

"It's not necessary."

"Of course it isn't." I followed her out of the house and down the walk to the driveway. It was windy and cold with a trace of dampness. Marcy didn't say anything on the way to the car and I didn't either. I could feel the chest-tightening coming on. I opened the door to the car for her and held it while she got in and smoothed the coat around her legs.

"Have a good date with the cultured man," I said.

"I ought to," Marcy said. "I really ought to."

"Do what you want to …"

"If you say that to me one more time, Jim …"

"You'll do what?"

"I'll go to some country-western bar and pick up the meanest looking red-neck there and let him screw my eyeballs out."

"Is this conversation necessary?" I asked.

"Not the last part of it. We should have had the first part of it months ago."

I edged the door in slowly. "I'll call you and if you're not busy with culture or red-necks we'll have dinner."

Marcy grabbed the door and jerked it closed. She kicked the engine over and threw it into reverse. Her front left tire rolled right over my right foot as she backed out of the driveway.

Art was still at the kitchen table. He watched me limp in and fought off a grin. "You and Marcy having a lovers' spat?"

"I don't have enough ambition to suit her." I tossed down the rest of the Stock. I put my right foot in one of the chair bottoms and felt the bones. It didn't seem to have any breaks.

"You're making a better living than I am," Art said. "Of course, I never ask how you do it."

"I'd never tell anyway." I took the foot out of the chair and put some weight on it. It was going to be stiff for a time. I poured a bit more Stock into my glass. "I've got to call Jack Smathers and wake him up. I don't think he's going to like it."

"We're going to want to talk to Peggy Holt's ex, this guy Simpson."

I nodded. I knew they would. In the bedroom I looked up Jack's home number and dialed it. Jack's wife, May, answered on the fifth or sixth ring. I'd never met her. Once, after he'd prosecuted a case I'd worked on, he got in his cups and talked about her. She sounded like a hard-ass woman. She'd been an operating room nurse when he'd met her and married her. She'd supported him through University of Georgia Law School and now that he'd decided the marriage might be a mistake she wasn't about to let him go without taking everything he had including the gold in his teeth.

"Jack has office hours," she said, "and he can be seen there. He needs his sleep like everybody else."

"Lady, I need my sleep too and if this wasn't important I'd be in my bed. So, how about giving him a chance to decide if he wants to talk to me?"

Jack sounded groggy for the first minute or so. The death of Harper jolted the sleep out of him. "This is getting rough."

I agreed and told him I thought we'd better get Edward Simpson back to Atlanta as soon as we could. The police would want to talk to him about his ex-wife and about how he'd spent the afternoon before he flew back to Chapel Hill.

"He says he just walked around town," Jack said.

"He'll have to convince the police of that." I threw the next hard lick at him, that I thought Maryann had been kidnapped by Harper and taken back by the mother or re-kidnapped by somebody else. I described the knit gloves I'd seen in the back of Harper's Impala.

"I'll see if Simpson can identify them."

"And we'll need some recent pictures of Maryann if he's got some."

"The gloves and the pictures ... got that." He said, before he hung up, that he'd call Simpson right away and he'd ring me back in a few minutes.

I went back into the kitchen and gave myself a final knock from the bottle. Art eased down and helped himself to about half a shot. I knew him pretty well and I knew he was looking at me as if he had some question or other that he wanted an answer for. It was there, just in back of his teeth, trying to push its way out.

"So ask it," I said.

"What?"

"The question," I said.

"Okay. What's in this one for you? The money's not good. Fifty or so a day isn't enough for you. I've got you and Hump figured some other way. You do the jobs that always seem to have some kind of gold chamber pot at the end. Right?"

"Boredom," I said. "Getting so I needed a job or I'd turn into an alcoholic."

"At your age it's a little late to worry about it. Now it's a race between skid row and the grave."

"I don't like either of those choices," I said.

"All the horseshit aside, it's the little girl, isn't it?"

"The kid's nothing to me."

"But it bothers you?"

I shrugged my shoulders at him. "She's in a box."

"A box?"

"The father's an ass with a new wife who probably hates the kid. God knows what the mother's like, but I've been getting some looks under the rocks. God bless the child with her as a mother. She'll need it."

"There's something else," Art said.

"You ever been in a tight spot where you were afraid?"

"A couple of times."

"Think how that kid feels. We're grown men but we pee in our pants under the gun. She's six years old, six years old."

"You trying to admit you've got a heart under all that shell?"

"No," I said. "I'm trying to tell you I've had too much to drink and I'm emotionally disturbed."

"I'll buy both of those."

The phone rang in the bedroom. It was Jack. He'd talked to Simpson and Simpson would be taking an early flight in from Chapel Hill. Jack was going to pick him up at Hartsfield. He wanted me to meet him at his office around ten-fifteen.

"The gloves?"

"He thinks they're Maryann's. He says they go with a red coat she was wearing the morning her mother took her from in front of the school."

I told Art about Simpson coming in and he said there'd be somebody from the department at Jack's office the next morning. And just to be sure he'd have the gloves brought along so that an exact identification could be made.

After he left it took me a long time to get to sleep. My right foot had a dull, faraway ache to it. If that wasn't enough Marcy seemed to have written me off completely. After loving me so long, so hard.

And nearer the surface the question that everybody wanted me to answer. Why I was willing to pick through all that dirty linen of wasted lives for fifty a day and expenses.

Goddamn the grown-ups anyway. I couldn't get that poor scared child out of my mind. In a few hours she'd seen as much of the dirty underside as most adults saw in a lifetime. The drugs, the greed and maybe even death. Somehow it didn't seem fair. And just before I fell over the edge something in me asked the hard question: whoever promised anybody that it was going to be fair?

When I entered Jack's office a bit after ten the next morning I didn't so much see Bear Hodge as smell him. I got a whiff of those two-for-a-quarters he smoked now and then and did a quick pivot to my right. He was sitting out of the sight line of the door, topcoat folded across his knees, chewing the last inch or so of the cigar.

"You got some business here, Hardman?"

"Maybe," I said. I ignored him for the next fifteen or twenty minutes. It was easy. The magazines were only three or four months old and now and then Jack's secretary would prance by.

That was enough to perk up the dead and I didn't consider myself dead yet.

Jack didn't so much walk into the office as he erupted into it. He didn't see Bear at first. "That son of a bitch didn't show," he shouted at me.

"Who didn't show?" Bear was on his feet, the topcoat trailing to the side, forgotten.

"My client, that ass Simpson. You know what he had the gall to do?"

"No, tell me," Bear said in that deceptively easy way.

"He called at the airport and had me paged. Gave me this cock and bull story about having some school work that just came up."

"He say when he would come?" Bear asked.

"As soon as he could."

Bear seemed to remember his topcoat. He reached down and picked it up and pushed his huge arms and shoulders into it. "I hope you're not playing games with me, Smathers."

"What do you mean by that?" The heat from Jack's anger with Simpson carried over and lashed at Bear.

"I mean we mean to ask this Simpson some questions. I don't want you to think you can get around me by advising him not to show up for the questioning."

"Just a fucking minute." Jack was moving toward Bear and that could be a bad mistake. Bear wasn't happy with the waste of a morning and if Jack pushed at him he'd get some lumps.

I edged over close, close but just out of the range of some wayward swing. "Keep it civilized, you two."

"Civilized, shit," Jack said. "If he wants to make that a formal charge, let him go ahead. I'll be glad to start a countersuit for damages."

"Call in a few more witnesses," Bear said. "I'll be glad to."

"Come on, you two," I said. "If this is a charade Jack's acting out, he went to a hell of a lot more trouble than he'd have had to. Bear, if you know Jack at all from his time with the D.A., you know this isn't his way of doing things."

Bear seemed to relax a bit so I decided to give him equal time. I turned the same kind of crap on Jack. "No matter what you think of Bear he's an honest cop and you know it. You've got to admit he's under bad pressure investigating the murder of his best friend's brother."

Jack nodded.

"Both of you have said some things you didn't mean. Right, Jack? Right, Bear?"

Grudgingly, still the hair up on their necks, they accepted my role as peacemaker. Jack turned to the blonde secretary who'd watched the near encounter with wide eyes and almost no breath and said, "Get me on a flight to Chapel Hill. Something around one o'clock."

"Make that two," I said.

"You paying your own way?" Jack asked.

"Yeah."

"Two then," Jack said, "and cancel all my appointments for the rest of the day." Jack gave Bear one more hard look before he went into the inner office and closed the door behind him.

Bear looked at me. "What's he going up there for?"

"My guess is he wants a deposition from Simpson."

"A lot of good that'd do," Bear said.

"It's the same thing you'd get out of him. A man wants to lie he can lie in Atlanta as well as Chapel Hill."

Bear was ready to leave but he was working on his exit line. The brush with Jack hadn't worked out the way he might have liked it to and he needed to add a few more points to his score.

"I hear you're finding a lot of bodies these days," he said.

"Just one," I said. "The one last night came and found me."

CHAPTER EIGHT

Chapel Hill's a town that hasn't really decided what it really wants to be. It's caught on the horns and can't decide which horn to be gored by. Around twenty years ago, when the student population at the University of North Carolina was down around seven or eight thousand, the town seemed to be offering itself as a kind of charming little village that never changes. The city ordinances perpetuated the small town charm by its emphasis upon the kinds of store fronts that could be constructed in the main central part of town and the size and type of signs.

In the last twenty years the student enrollment has gone over the twenty thousand mark and the small village charm just isn't there anymore. Swarms of real estate dealers are mucking around the fringes and it looks like the rest of the battle is just a delaying action.

The limousine from the airport dropped us off at the Carolina Inn a little before two-thirty. On directions from the driver we walked the long block down to Franklin and Columbia and found an outside phone booth. I waited outside while Jack called Simpson's home number. He talked with Simpson's wife. She said that he was either back in the stacks at the library or at the graduate instructors' office at Bingham Hall. She gave Jack a set of directions that were supposed to lead us across campus. The step by step instructions didn't work. They were given in terms of other buildings we didn't know either. And couldn't find.

It took us about twenty minutes. Finally one of the students turned and pointed. "Bingham's right there."

It was a large office with perhaps two dozen desks in it. Each desk had its low partition, but you could stand at the entrance and look across the room and see the faces of the instructors. Edward Simpson was at a desk in the far left corner. His head was down and he appeared to be grading papers.

Jack and I made our way past some startled and curious students and instructors. I guess we looked too old to be enrolled in freshman English. Simpson didn't see us until we stopped in front of his desk.

"We thought we'd better have a talk with you," Jack said.

"Look," Simpson began, "I'm sorry about this morning, but ..."

"I need two things from you and neither of them is an apology," Jack said. "You've got me in an awkward position with the Atlanta police and you're going to get me out of it, willingly or unwillingly. I don't like being accused of advising a client not to appear for a police questioning."

"What do you want?"

"A deposition that covers yesterday's routine, what you did and where you went."

"Okay," Simpson said, "what do I do?"

"First," Jack said, "we find a poor lawyer who needs some work."

The office in the rear of a second floor of a building on Rosemary Street was old but the furnishings and the law books were new and so was the lawyer, Arnold Hopkins. He'd just passed the North Carolina Bar exam a year or so before and it looked like nobody knew about it yet. Hopkins acted like we'd given him his birthday present a few months early and hurried down the hall to find the secretary he and a couple of other young lawyers shared. She was thin as a rake handle and homely so that threw out one way of killing the dull time.

Simpson was about three minutes into his recitation of how he'd spent the afternoon of Monday, January 15th when Jack interrupted him. "Let's start over," he said. "I never liked sight-seeing on Peachtree. It's worth shit as an alibi." He turned to the secretary who was blushing over her steno pad. "Tear those notes up." He whirled on Simpson and snarled at him. "I didn't come up here to hear fairy tales. I didn't cancel four appointments to hear you get creative with me."

"I'm telling the truth," Simpson said.

"You believe him, Hardman?" Jack asked me.

"About as much as I believe in Santa Claus. Maybe a bit less."

"Start with around 11:15. You left my office where you'd been talking with me and Jim Hardman." He nodded at the secretary. "And this time tell the fucking truth."

"I can't tell the truth," Simpson said. "If it got back to my wife ..."

"It won't leave this room here in Chapel Hill. Mr. Hopkins and his secretary are officers of the court and they know the penalties for divulging information."

Hopkins didn't like the tone of that, the threat in it, but he nodded at Simpson.

"And the police in Atlanta will just check it out. If it checks out that'll be the end of it."

"If it got in the papers it would ruin my marriage."

"I'll make sure it doesn't."

I felt I'd better encourage him. "I'll check it out first myself. If you're telling the truth I'll prove it and pass it on to a cop on the force who's a friend of mine."

The secretary poised her pencil over the steno pad and waited. Jack put his back to Simpson and lowered one eyelid at me, his way of thanking me for jumping in and helping.

It wasn't a thing he usually did, Simpson said. He'd never done it before, even when the P.M.L.A. met in New York. Atlanta was different. It had a kind of boom town feeling to it, almost a lusty quality. As soon as he left Jack's office he decided that he wanted a woman. It just hit him standing out on Forsyth. Here he was in a big city, sensing the excitement, and he wanted a woman. Oh, he knew that usually happened at night. Even the driver of the cab he flagged down hadn't believed it at first. It wasn't even noon yet. Simpson convinced the driver and the driver parked at the service station and made a few calls. When he returned he drove Simpson to a duplex on Howell Mill Road. Simpson didn't know the number. It was sort of brown stucco with white trim and quite a bit of shrubbery in the front yard. The girl there didn't believe Simpson either. She was hardly awake when he arrived. He'd stayed with the woman until an hour before plane time and he'd caught a cab and picked up his luggage at the Sheraton and barely reached Hartsfield in time for his flight to Raleigh-Durham.

And that, according to Simpson, was the whole truth.

Jack was satisfied. He told the secretary to type it up and we'd be back in thirty or forty minutes to get Simpson's signature on it and get it witnessed.

"What now?" Simpson asked when we were out on Rosemary Street.

"Where's the police station?" I asked.

Simpson looked stunned. "I told the truth back there."

"Hear him out," Jack said to Simpson.

"Where's the police station?"

"Down there. Rosemary and North Columbia."

I turned toward Simpson and we walked in the direction of the police station. I spread it out for him hard and simple. Maybe it had been the right thing not to report that Maryann had been kidnapped when it was fairly certain that his ex-wife had the child. Now it wasn't that simple. It looked like Maryann was a pawn in a drug war. She'd been kidnapped once and then taken away from that kidnapper. While we thought there was a chance that his ex-wife had Maryann now we weren't sure of that. The kidnappers believed they had a kind of immunity. The ex-wife couldn't bring charges. If Maryann was being held by somebody else they probably felt very safe. It was time to take the safety away from them. I wanted Simpson, along with Jack as his lawyer, to go in and report the kidnapping. He was to tell it the way it was and then explain that he'd decided to report it because there was a chance that someone other than his ex-wife had taken the child.

"I don't see what good that does," Simpson said.

"The police don't investigate rumors of a kidnapping, but they do look for kidnapped children. And the F.B.I, comes into it too."

"Hardman convinced me on the flight up," Jack said.

"If you think it's what I ought to do."

Jack said it was.

I got directions from Simpson to a beer place, The Shack, about a third of a block from the police station. I watched them go into the police station and then I went down to The Shack and had a few beers and a sandwich while I waited for them.

An hour later we went back to Hopkins' office and Simpson read the deposition and signed it and Hopkins and one of the lawyers from down the hall signed it as witnesses. While Simpson and I waited out in the hall Jack wrote a check to cover Hopkins' time and his fee.

"I've got to go back to Bingham," Simpson said when Jack joined us.

"We'll walk that way with you," Jack said.

"Both of you have been very hard on me today," Simpson said as we turned off North Columbia onto Franklin Street.

Jack didn't say anything right away. He was looking into windows and at Jeff's Campus Confectionery he caught Simpson by the elbow and guided him through the door. "I can use a beer. How about you, Jim?"

"I can stand another."

We stood around the beer counter in back and sipped at our beer while Simpson drank a coke. "What did you mean back there?" Jack asked.

"Well," he said, almost stuttering, "you two are acting like this is all my fault. And it's not." He turned to me. "I thought you were going to find Maryann. That's what I was paying you to do."

"I found her," I said evenly. "And I found her a lot faster than I thought I could. Rather, I found where she should have been. I hadn't planned on being right in the middle of two murders. Your ex-wife isn't very neat with other people's lives."

"Are you still working for me?"

"Until I find Maryann. After that, I don't think so."

Simpson dipped into his inside jacket pocket and brought out his check book. While Jack and I looked at each other and drank our beer Simpson wrote out a check and passed it to Jack. On its way past me I saw that it was for a thousand dollars. Jack folded it and put it in his wallet.

"That's for Mr. Hardman, his fee and his expenses." He showed us an embarrassed grin. "I'm going to have a hell of a time just trying to explain these expenses to my wife. I don't think she approves of what I'm doing."

"I didn't tell you," Jack said, "but Hardman here has a friend working on this with him."

"I don't care," Simpson said. "Hire half the city if you have to. All I want is for you to find Maryann."

"I'll find her," I said.

"Maybe you think, from the way I've been acting, that I don't love Maryann. That's not true. She's the only good thing that came out of a bad marriage. It's just that my new wife resents her. That makes it bad around the house. Maybe just for a few hours I tried to tell myself that it might be better if Maryann stayed with her mother. I don't think so now."

"At least that's honest," Jack said.

"I guess I don't like to face a problem. I think I believe that if I don't it'll just go away."

We drank our beer in an easier silence. I still couldn't say that I liked Simpson, but now I thought I understood him better. An hour later we were on a flight back to Atlanta.

It wasn't a hard house to find. I drove slowly up Howell Mill Road, watching both sides of the street, and then, there it was just like Simpson had described it. A brown stucco duplex with white trim and some hedges and what he hadn't remembered, a mock orange tree. I parked behind a white '72 Ventura and took my time getting out. I wrote down the license plate numbers and left them in the glove box.

One more thing to check. He'd said, when I'd questioned him, that the woman, or girl, had red hair and a beauty mark on her left cheek. And she'd been about five-ten. My job was just to check that part of Simpson's story. If that matched, the rest of it was up to Art or Bear or one of the other detectives.

I didn't like putting the girl out of work. Still, she'd only miss a night or two and she might have to move. That didn't seem to be much of a problem with the prosties. It seemed to be part of the drill. Every new girl in town was old in some other town.

I pressed the lighted door bell I didn't have to wait long. The woman who came to the door answered the description exactly. The red hair, the beauty mark, real or false, and the height. She wore a short white linen dress that didn't hide much. And, watching her sway slightly in the doorway, I decided she'd been in the booze or some grass or hash.

"Come in," she said. "I'm not doing a thing for the next hour or so."

I didn't. The play for pay had dulled some for me. From her point of view I guess I looked like I was hesitating from shyness.

"Didn't Frankie send you?"

I shook my head. "I'm looking for my cousin, Annabelle Morris. I thought she lived here."

"Well, she doesn't." She backed out of the doorway and slammed the door in my face.

I called Art at home as soon as I got to my house. He said he'd have somebody from Vice check the place out later. If they could bust her with a john they could use that to peel the facts about Simpson out of her. With one charge against her a statement about Simpson wouldn't matter.

"I've been trying to call you all day."

It was Marcy on the phone and she'd caught me in the shower. I was dripping all over the floor and the bed. I decided it was time to change the sheets anyway.

"How's Mr. Wonderful?" I asked.

"Who?"

"The cultured gentleman. My opposite."

"He's fine. Where were you all day?"

"You want the whole story?"

Marcy said she did.

I shook a cigarette out of the pack on the nightstand and put my wet behind on the bed. I lit the cigarette. "I was over at Jack Smathers and I kept him and Bear from trying to kill each other. That was so much fun that I flew up to Chapel Hill and helped browbeat one of Jack's clients, the guy who's the father of the little girl. And then we flew back to Atlanta and I went over to see a red-haired whore on business."

"Your business or hers?"

"A bit of both," I said. "You see, she had this hour to kill and I wasn't doing anything…"

"Oh, shut up, Jim."

I did. I waited about thirty seconds and when she hadn't said anything else I said, "I looked in the entertainment section this morning and didn't find any ballet or concerts, but there are some great foreign films and you could take turns translating to each other."

"What?"

"Well, I understand the subtitles don't really tell you what they're saying."

"Jim, you're an ass," Marcy said, but there was a chuckle somewhere back in her throat.

"I guess I am. You've got to admit though that I wasn't the one who started talking about having found some cultured woman who loved heavy music and ballet."

"I'm cultured and I like music and ballet."

"Maybe we could have a date some night," I said.

"Tonight?"

"I'd like to but I can't."

"That's what I get for putting my pride aside. I guess the red-haired whore has another hour to kill."

"Marcy, this is going to sound harder than I mean it to. I've got to find that little girl. Put you and me aside for a moment. See if you can remember how it was to be six years old and scared to death."

"All right, Jim."

"I might drop by late for a drink if we run into a dead end."

"I'll be here if I don't go out and pick up that red-neck," she said.

"I'll call before I come by."

"Do that."

The phone went dead at my ear.

Hump made the call to Ernie, the Wildwood Connector, from my place. Ernie didn't want to see us again. Hump kept insisting. Ernie hung up on him once but Hump dialed him right back.

I had my ear next to the receiver and I heard Ernie say, "White child's nothing to me."

"Screw the grown-ups," Hump said. "Children don't pick their parents."

"Come on over," Ernie said after a long silence.

CHAPTER NINE

Ernie was exactly where we'd left him the last time. There was an open quart of Bud on the coffee table in front of him and three plastic cups. "What now?" he asked before we were all the way through the doorway.

"You offering beer or are you expecting two other people?" Hump said.

Ernie poured each of us a cup of beer. "All right, now I've done the social crap. What else you want besides my beer?"

"You been following the adventures of Peggy Holt in the papers?"

"Some," he said.

"A new chapter," Hump said. "A small timer died on Hardman's doorstep last night. We think he'd kidnapped the girl. Now somebody else has her or Peggy has her."

"The child's nothing to me."

"You said that before," Hump said.

"I'll say it again if you want me to."

"Other news," I said. "The dead man had an $8 bag in his sock. High grade stuff. You reckon it might be some of her dope?"

"It might."

"I think the child's trade bait. Her for the dope."

"Unless Peggy's got her," Ernie said. "What you want from me?"

"I want the name of somebody who works with her, somebody who'll get a message to her from me."

"You think I'm crazy?"

I shook my head.

Ernie got up from the sofa and limped away, his back to me. "You think I'm going around giving out names? You know how long I'd last in town doing that?"

"Not long," I admitted.

"Damned right," he said. "That's the first smart thing you've said since you pranced your white ass in here."

"All we want is a name," Hump said. "A name we can pass a question through to her. Is the kid with her or does somebody else have her?"

"That's all?"

"Just a question. No cops. No tail when we meet him."

"Your word, Hump?"

"My word," Hump said.

Ernie limped over to the bedroom entrance. "Stay here and drink your beer. Don't get anywhere near my door." He went into the bedroom and closed the door behind him.

I sat on the sofa next to Hump. "I think he's getting tired of us."

"With damn good reason," Hump said. "I'm getting tired of us myself."

Ernie came out of the bedroom. "You know the Crystal on Peachtree and Seventh?"

"I know it," I said.

"He'll be at the front counter, the one facing the street. He'll be wearing a red velvet jacket and blue jeans."

"Is he black?" Hump asked.

"Black," Ernie said. "And in case you're trying to shit me he won't be carrying anything."

"We're not shitting you," Hump said.

"Goodbye then."

"No charge this time?" I headed for the door.

"My charge is you don't come back … ever."

I went on out the door. Hump remained behind. "What if I need some smoke some night?"

"I'll think on that between now and then," Ernie said.

He was there, sipping a paper cup of coffee and looking down into the empty bowl that had had chili in it. There were empty seats on both sides of him. Hump sat down on his right and I went over to the counter and bought two cups of coffee. When I sat on the black's left he didn't even look around at me. Hump hadn't wasted any time.

"I don't know any Peggy Holt," the black was saying.

"That's all right," Hump said, soft and easy. "This is just pretend. If you did know a Peggy Holt, maybe you could get a message to her and have her call Mr. Hardman here."

"If I did," he said.

"That's all I want," Hump said.

I got out my pad and wrote down my name and phone number. I put it on the counter next to his cup of coffee. He looked at it and looked back out at the movement on the street.

"Big rush on this," I said.

"Not my problem," he said. "I don't know any Peggy Holt."

An hour later the phone rang in my bedroom.

It was a woman's voice, low and throaty. "You wanted me to call you?"

"I need to talk to you."

"Talk fast," she said.

"Is Maryann with you?"

"Are you putting me on?"

I asked what she meant.

"Don't you have her? Isn't that why you wanted me to call you?"

"We've got our wires crossed," I said. "I'm working for your ex."

"Doing what?"

"Trying to find Maryann."

"I'm not sure I can believe you. I believed a couple of people in the last day or two and they didn't turn out to be what they said they were."

"Call your ex in Chapel Hill and ask him about me. Then call me back."

She hung up. She called back in ten minutes. "I don't know if I can trust you."

"I want to see you," I said. "I'm not a cop and I won't bring the cops with me."

"Edward said he didn't know you very well," she said.

"That's true."

"What do you think of Edward?"

"I think he's a gutless asshole," I said.

Peggy laughed, deep and warm and I could feel the hairs straighten on the back of my neck. "There's a pay phone outside the quick food store…a 7-11 I think…near the corner of Virginia and Highland. Be there at exactly 9:30. The phone will ring at exactly 9:35. The call will be for you and you'll get instructions then."

"We have to go through all this run-around?"

"Or not at all," she said.

"Done," I said and hung up.

I got down to Virginia and Highland a few minutes early and spent the time driving around the block. At 9:29 I pulled into the almost empty parking lot in front of the store. Through the wide plate-glass window I watched a few people browsing through the overpriced foodstuffs. A minute or so before 9:35, I rolled down the window on the driver's side and felt the sting of cold wind on my face.

At 9:35 the phone rang. I got out of the car and hurried over to the phone. As I reached for the receiver a car, pulling into the parking area, lit me with its headlights. I turned and saw it stop in the space on the other side of my car. Then the phone was to my ear.

"Hello."

"Are you Mr. Hardman?" It was a man's voice.

"Yes."

"Are you alone?"

"Yes," I said.

"You'd better be," the man said.

"I'm waiting," I said. He didn't answer and then I felt a touch on my shoulder. It was sucker time for me, I guess. I turned and there she was, Peggy Holt. She reached past me and took the receiver.

"It's okay," she said into the phone and hung it up.

"My car or yours?" she asked.

"That's the question that gets asked at Uncle Sam's bar," I said.

"I don't have much time," she said. "And no time at all for jokes."

"Either," I said.

"Mine," she said.

Beside her, on the way to her car, I got my long look at her. She wore a pair of tan jeans that looked like she'd bought them tight and then shrunk them to skin tight in the shower. I couldn't get a good look at her upper body. She was wearing a Navy pea coat, one of the good old ones that went back to the Korean war or before. She was wearing desert boots for women, the heavy ones that I guess you could call walking boots. They didn't hurt her grace at all.

What threw me off stride some was the hair. I'd been expecting long flowing hair. Instead she was wearing a kind of round and flat black hat, what you might call a woman's riding derby.

RALPH DENNIS

At least, I remember seeing them in a couple of films. Her hair'd been stuffed up into the hat, I thought, unless she'd had it cut.

It was all there and I could feel it. The knowing sexuality, but it wasn't the brassy kind, the type that came with too much knowledge. It wasn't the whore's knowledge of what it was worth and what could be done with it. That was missing but, for me, it was still there and I knew how people like Ernie and Jack Smathers could be damaged by her. I don't know how she did it but the sexuality had the shock of a kind of purity in it. Like a choir girl who had it and knew she did and didn't know what to do with it.

Even though I knew better I felt a scrotum tightening that didn't have anything to do with the temperature. And I told myself to quit it, this one will eat your liver and lights and do it just on instinct. It won't even be personal to her.

Her skin, as I'd expected, in the inside light with the door to her Fairlane open, was almost blue-white, like fresh milk. Then she closed the door and backed out of the parking space. She turned into Highland and went the one long block and when we were in front of the church she made a left into Los Angeles. She stayed on Los Angeles until it split and curved to the right and became Brookridge Drive. She kept bearing to her left and then we were passing Orme Park. It was only about two city blocks long and about a half block wide. There was a slide and a few swings and a shallow stream that ran through the center of it. I'd been avoiding this area for a couple of months. The last time I'd been at Orme Park was the morning Art had taken me there to identify the body of Heddy, the red-haired topless dancer who'd been involved with some others in the J.C. Cartway fight-robbery. She'd been there, face down in the stream with her throat cut.

Peggy pulled to the curb and parked near the area where the fountain and the slide and the swings were. "Would you like to walk around some?" she asked.

"Why not?"

It was silly, it was stupid. It was pretty damn cold to be sitting out in a two-person swing. I got out my cigarettes and offered her one and lit them by shielding them against the gusting wind. Blowing the smoke out it was hard to tell which was the smoke and which the breath condensation.

"Where do I start?" Peggy braced her legs, pushed off and set the swing in motion.

"Where's Maryann?"

"I don't know. She was outside and that man, the one who'd been following me, took her yesterday afternoon."

"Outside where?"

"It doesn't matter."

"Who has her now?" I asked.

"I thought you did." She reached into her pea jacket pocket and brought out a small scrap of newsprint. "This was in the *Journal,* in the personals section."

"When?"

"Today."

I got out my lighter and read it by the flicker and whip of the flame.

Lost girl doll. Will return for
valuable consideration. Answer
Journal Box 44B.

I capped the flame and handed the newsprint back to her. "What makes you think they mean Maryann?"

"Some of the dealers use the personals column. It's fluid out there on the street, people moving, changing addresses, no phones where they can be reached."

"So they'd assume you'd read it?"

"Yes."

"You answer it yet?"

"I will tomorrow," she said.

I dropped my cigarette and ground it into the dirt. The sparks flew for yards downwind. "What do they want from you?"

"I can't say."

"I think I know," I said. "And there must be a hell of a lot of it for them to go to this trouble. For people to kill for it."

"I can't say."

"You going to make the deal?"

She didn't answer right away. She flipped the cigarette toward the stream. "I still don't know if I can trust you."

"So far no cops," I said.

"I'm frightened."

"Why?" The tremor was in her voice and I'd had to brace myself against it.

"Some of the people in this with me don't want to give it up. It's worth too much. They're saying it's my child, not theirs."

"What do they want you to do?"

"They want me to set up a meeting. They'll try to get Maryann back without giving it up."

"You set up a meeting with Harper?" I asked.

"If you mean did I set him up so he'd be killed, the answer is no."

"You got any idea who got to him?"

"No. But it must have been somebody big in the drug traffic. They want to shut us down."

That might be Raymond or somebody Raymond did his dealing through. It didn't sound like something Raymond would do, but I couldn't say the same for some of the people working for him. At that level the animals take over. Claws and teeth and all.

"The next big question. What happened to Randy King? The police think he found out you were dealing and you killed him to shut him up."

"That's a laugh." She didn't laugh. "You know where the stuff came from? Randy furnished it."

"Where'd he get it?"

"I can't say."

"What happened to him?"

"I left the apartment about noon. I had to meet somebody. I was gone about an hour and a half, almost two hours. When I came back I found him like that ... in the kitchen."

"Anything missing from the apartment?"

"I didn't stay to look," she said. "Anyway, what they wanted wasn't there."

"You have a gun?"

"No."

"Could it have been some of the people working with you ... wanting to cut down on the number of people sharing in it?"

"I don't think so. You see, Randy said he could get some more from the same place. It would have been stupid to kill him and cut off the source."

We sat, slowly moving backwards and forward, like lovers trying to figure the next con. Silent with all the brain cells going at quick step. All around us house lights were going out. Now and then a car would rip and tear around the oval road that ran around the park. For the kids I guess it was sort of a raceway.

"How are you going to handle it?" I asked.

"I don't know. I'll have to send a letter to the *Journal* and see what we can arrange."

"You people are kids at this. I'd make a guess they're pros. A trick is the first thing they'd expect out of you."

"They say it can be done," she said.

"Don't make any bets on it."

She put a toe into the grooved track in front of the swing and dug in. We stopped. She turned and I got another scent of her. "Are you a pro?"

"I used to be," I said.

"You could help me get her back if you wanted to."

"Maybe."

"Would you?"

I could feel the trembling start in her leg, the one that brought the swing to a stop and now was holding us in mid-swing. She bent her knee and we were moving again.

"I won't work for you. I wouldn't even if the police weren't looking for you. I'm working for your ex and I don't care much for him either. If I get Maryann it goes to the court. The court decides."

"The way things are now, it might be better if Edward had her," she said.

"I'll handle it on my terms."

"What terms?"

"That you get the answer delivered and then you and all your friends stay out of it. I don't want any freelance messing it up."

"All right."

"I mean it. If I look around and find some cowboy following me I quit and go home."

"I said I agreed."

I got up and stamped my feet. They were going numb. I came back to the swing and faced her. "How are you sending your answer?"

"Mail," she said.

I shook my head. "If we're going to the trouble to stake the place out and set up a follow, I want to be sure there's something for them to pick up."

"I'll send it over by a friend."

I arched my back, stretching the muscles, trying to get some heat inside my topcoat. "I'll need to know who's bringing it, what they look like."

"He'll be young, black and wearing a black hat with a silver band."

"Around eleven o'clock?"

She said yes.

"Let's walk some," I said. "I'm freezing. We stopped on the narrow footbridge. I looked down at the dark water. "The bad thing,

Peggy, is that you're going to have to be prepared to go through with it. To go along with whatever deal you offer in your letter. If they're smart the pick-up man won't lead us anywhere. It'll be a dead end. That happens you'll have to buy Maryann back."

"I understand. I don't think the others will like it."

I stepped around her and headed back to the car. When she was beside me I said, "I'll need some way to get in touch with you."

"There'll be someone at the Crystal all day tomorrow. Sitting at the counter. With a copy of Hip magazine."

She had very little more to say. She didn't even say goodnight when she dropped me at the 7-11 store.

I drove out to Marcy's apartment without calling. All the lights were out and I didn't see her car in the parking area out front. I didn't even try the door bell. I drove back across town to my house. It was falling apart and the sad heavy blues were playing in my head.

I should have had my mind on the business at hand. I parked in the driveway and was headed up the walk toward the unlighted front porch when the two men stepped out of the shadows at the far corner of the house. The one closest to me, a short, rather slim man, showed the gun. That nailed me to the walk. When they moved closer I saw that both of them had scarves wrapped around the lower part of their faces and hats pulled down low over their eyes.

I was still trying to decide what my best move was when the larger man, the one who wasn't showing a gun, stepped past the smaller man and hit me twice in the belly. As I was falling he stepped up closer and clubbed me on the side of the head.

I was dry-heaving but I wasn't out. The one with the gun leaned over and spoke through his scarf. It muffled his voice and made it sound like it was coming through a mouthful of oatmeal.

"Stay out of it, Hardman."

I coughed and tasted bile in the back of my throat.

The larger man bent over me. "You hear him, speak up."

I coughed again.

"Speak up."

I wanted to say something but I was afraid I was going to vomit.

"I think he's going to lose his supper," the smaller man said. He moved away and I lost him in the darkness. "Finish it," he said.

I caught the first kick low in the ribs on my right side. I tried to roll away from the second and it him me on the point of my hip. The man doing the kicking was grunting with the effort and when he was directly above me and the sky behind him I could see the spray and spurt of condensation.

There was a third and a fourth kick and I knew he was working his way up to my head. I got my arms up and tried to protect my face. I caught one kick on my shoulder and another across a forearm.

I quit counting the kicks. Some of them seemed like echoes anyway and when I thought I was going to lose it all and go under the man back in the shadows, the one with the gun said, "That's enough."

After they left... I didn't even try to turn and see what they were driving... I lay out there on the frozen ground, grunting and whimpering. It took me a long time to decide whether I wanted to live or die. I don't remember what it was I decided, but I found myself crawling on all fours up the front steps.

I don't think I set an Olympic record for getting the front' door open. I think it took me half an hour.

CHAPTER TEN

"They only kicked the ugly parts of you," Hump said. "I assume they tried for the pretty parts and you didn't let them close."

I don't think that Hump was in a very good mood. It wasn't that he hadn't wanted to help, but he was puffing into the phone when we talked and I had enough sense left to realize that I'd caught him about thigh-deep in some business. So I'd said he didn't have to come, that he could send Marsh Whitman if he could find him.

"The shit you say," he'd said. And he'd come, though it had taken him some time to find Whitman. Whitman was a black underground "doctor", a young black who'd almost finished medical school before he'd gotten into some kind of trouble and dropped out. For a hundred or so he'd fix a gunshot wound or a cutting. For a poor black that couldn't afford to pay it was free.

Whitman had used about a roll of tape on my ribs and he'd poked and prodded me until I was sweating and clenching my teeth. Before he went into the kitchen to have a drink he said he thought I had a couple of floating ribs, ribs that had almost been kicked loose. "You ought to take it easy for a few days," he said.

Hump came back from pouring him a drink and sat on the edge of the bed. "You know them?"

"No." I'd started to shake my head but it hurt too much.

"Somebody worried about their faces being seen. Wonder why?"

"Past me," I said.

"Not your usual one-shot hardasses. Not the type that take their fifty dollars and disappear into the woodwork."

"The two the old lady told us about," I said. "In size they'd match the two that were at Harper's apartment when he had Maryann with him."

Hump nodded. "Not shy with her, but shy with you. Think on that."

I tried the whole time I was alone in the house, while Hump was dropping off Whitman. It didn't come to anything, so I stored it away in the "loose ends" section of my mind.

Art came by as soon as he could get away.

"You talked to her and you just let her walk away?"

"She drove away," I said. "Hell, Art, it was the only way I could talk to her."

"If somebody hadn't already kicked the crap out of you, I'd be tempted."

I let the anger run out of him before I went on to tell him what Peggy had told me about the murder of Randy King. He made me repeat what she'd said about Randy furnishing the stuff and her assertion that her people hadn't killed Randy, that it would have been foolish because he'd said he could furnish a lot more.

"You thinking what I am?" Art asked.

"Where does a young cop get a lot of dope?"

"He makes a big bust and doesn't turn the stuff in and he doesn't make the arrest. Just scares the shit out of the one he busts or maybe uses some muscle."

"But he wasn't working narcotics," I said.

"I'll have to check this out," Art said. "Until we know for sure this stays in this room."

"Done," I said.

Hump shook his head. He hadn't followed us. It was just as well. Neither of us wanted to explain.

But Art couldn't shake it. It rankled him and turned him sour. It carried over and almost messed up my plans for the next day. He heard me out.

"So you make this agreement that we'll pull her chestnuts out of the fire? We do her scut work and she goes right on selling that crap on the street."

"That might be the price," I said.

"It's too high."

"Other benefits," I said. "If we can believe her, the people who have the kid now are the ones who probably killed Randy King and the Harper guy."

"And if she's lying to us, we find the kid and that's all?"

"Maybe," Hump said. "Even if we find the kid and that's all, it's still worth it."

"To you, maybe."

"What does that mean?"

"You're being paid to find her," Art said. "It's nothing to me."

"Check the new stuff over at the department," I said. "You're going to find that Edward Simpson reported a kidnapping up in Chapel Hill. He did it this afternoon."

"You have a hand in that?"

I nodded. "From the way you talk one would think you didn't have kids."

"Don't try that con on me."

"We'll do it without you. Everybody knows the cops are more interested in busting whores than solving murders and kidnappings."

"Like it or not, you know damned well I'm coming."

"A man of instant decision," Hump said.

"Why?" I asked.

"Why am I a man of instant … ?" Art began.

"Why are you in?"

"Without me you two could screw it up," Art said.

We decided upon the drill and Art said he could furnish the walkie-talkies and a policewoman. He left, yawning, and saying that he had to return to the department and think up some excuse so he could get a couple of hours of sleep.

Hump bedded down on the sofa.

Twice before I went to bed I started dialing Marcy's number. Each time, five digits into it, I changed my mind. It didn't seem worthwhile.

At nine-thirty Hump dropped me in front of the *Journal-Constitution* building. He'd work his way over to the Apco parking building across the street and try to use a twenty to buy him a position in the driveway on the lower level so that he could see the main entrance of the building.

It was a new building, one the papers had just moved into, but it looked like it had been built on top of a World War II pill box. I went in and found Art at the security desk. He was leaning on the counter talking to the guard and looking at the two decks of TV monitors that wrapped halfway around the security area. He saw me and pushed away from the counter and showed me some red-rimmed eyes.

"Let me show you around," he said.

"How does it look?"

"Like Oak Ridge," he said. "Better than I thought."

"We could use a break or two."

Art led me to the bank of elevators. They were on our left as we faced outside, to the right of anyone as they entered. "Only one way out through here. On the fourth floor you could exit through the shop area. But there's a guard there and you need *Journal-Constitution* identification to get past the guard. If our man, after he picks up the letter, gets on the elevator we alert the guard up there to turn him back."

He turned me and we walked past the security guard, down a hallway past the Personnel office and the Payroll office. At the end of the hall there was a single elevator. "This goes from the underground parking lot to any of the floors upstairs. A news story breaks, a reporter gets on the elevator and rides it down to the underground garage, gets in one of the press cars."

"Might be a way our man could get out," I said.

Art shook his head. "No chance at all. That security guard up there with the monitors has one that shows him anyone trying to enter the underground parking and one that shows him anyone trying to drive out that way. And he's the one that opens and closes the only door to the garage." We walked back up the hall to the security desk. "If our man starts down this hall the guard'll stop him and turn him back."

"He's bottlenecked. Only one way in and one way out."

"Beautiful, huh?"

We passed the security desk and turned right. We were at the Want Ad counter. A dark-haired girl in a blue pants suit moved up to the counter to meet us. I'd opened my mouth to say that I didn't want to place an ad when Art laughed. "You know how we used to say that all policewomen wore army shoes? Times change."

The dark-haired girl smiled and held out her hand. "I'm Mary Barton."

"I take it all back," I said.

"Unless Peggy plays a game on us we'll know when the answer to the ad gets here. The black hat with the silver band. The really important one is when the pick-up's made. I'll be at the security desk, obviously a businessman who's trying to see someone upstairs. And having some trouble getting there."

"You look like a businessman who went to an orgy last night," I said.

"It happens," Art said. "Now, when our man asks Mary for the mail for 44B she's going to hit a trouble button that will light up on the board at the security desk. No sound or anything, just a light that comes on."

I nodded. It sounded good so far.

"As soon as the light goes on I'll leave the security desk and go over to the bank of elevators up by the front entrance. I'll get my look at the pick-up man. If he tries to move toward the back elevator the guard'll turn him back. If he gets on the front elevators I'll ride with him and see what floor he goes to. My guess is he'll go back out the front entrance. If he does that I'll reach you on the walkie-talkie and give you a description. If he's on foot you follow him and Hump tails both of you in the car. If he's picked up out front you tail him in Hump's car and we'll play leapfrog."

"Looks good."

I followed Art back to the security desk. The guard handed him an attaché case. Art opened it and handed me a walkie-talkie in a brown paper sack. "I'll give you a minute to get across to the parking deck and well test these."

I waved at Mary Barton and went outside and crossed to the Apco parking deck. Hump was parked there with his nose almost out on the street. The walkie-talkies checked out and we settled in for the long wait.

By my watch a couple of minutes after eleven Hump tapped me on the shoulder. "The black dude there."

I turned and looked down Marietta in the direction of Five Points. The young black was on the other side of the street, on the corner, waiting for the light to change. He was wearing a black hat with a wide silver band. "At least that part of it's on time."

When the light changed the black sprinted off the curb like coming out of the blocks. He slowed down in front of First Georgia Bank, passed the narrow vacant lot at a slow walk, and stopped before the entrance to the *Journal-Constitution* building. He seemed to be hesitating, like he didn't want to go in.

"Move it," Hump said in a low whisper next to me.

If it was a matter of nerves, the young black shook it off after a few seconds. He straightened his back and went in.

He was grinning to himself when he came out two or three minutes later. He stopped and looked around. The grin stayed there and he swaggered down Marietta toward Five Points.

"Free at last," Hump said. "You see, he thought somebody was going to put an arm on him in there."

The walkie-talkie crackled at us. "The letter's here," Art said.

"Yeah," I answered, "saw it delivered."

"Stand by."

Noon came. The foot traffic on Marietta got thicker. The office workers on their lunch break or off to the banks. It would be this way for another hour or so. If I was planning the pick-up it would be my time, the situation I'd choose. It worked for you and against you. The pick-up man might be able to lose a tail better on a crowded street. He could hurl himself into crowds, bury himself in sheer numbers. On the other hand, the tail wasn't as obvious. The pick-up man would have trouble isolating the tail. On an almost empty street it was child-simple.

"What you think?" Hump asked.

I shook my head. If they had figured the angles it wasn't worth a guess. It was a matter of personal choice. Stand on the fence and jump either way. I'd option for the crowd. They might go for the relatively empty street.

Twelve-thirty. Twelve-forty-five.

"Pick-up," Art said over the walkie-talkie. "Heading out the front right now. Longish blond hair, six feet tall, wearing a gray, double knit suit, dark tie."

"There he is," Hump said.

"Got him," I said into the walkie-talkie.

He was a big guy, broad shoulders and girl waisted. His hair long but not freaky long, just modish. Hair didn't stir in the wind out there, probably sprayed.

"What's he doing?" Art asked.

"Just standing out front. Looking around."

"Make it," Art said.

"I don't think he's a walker."

"The green Electra," Hump said.

A green Electra slowed as it covered the last few yards. It pulled to a stop. The pick-up man, instead of getting into the passenger seat, walked around the front of the Electra and opened the door on the driver's side. I didn't get a good look at the original driver. He looked like a young kid, someone in his late teens.

I called Art and read him the plate numbers.

"Keep in touch," Art said. "I'll catch up soon as I can."

Hump kicked the engine over. "Give him a start, half a block or so."

The green Electra pulled away from the curb heading toward Five Points. I waited until it reached the corner of Forsyth and Marietta. It caught a red light. I nodded at Hump and Hump eased across the street and into the proper lane. We were six or seven cars behind.

"Heading toward Five Points," I said into the walkie-talkie.

"Be right behind you," Art said. "My car's coming around front now."

The light changed and the Electra angled over and worked over into the right hand turn lane. Hump followed his lead. "I think he's turning onto Peachtree, headed for Whitehall."

"I've got wheels," Art said.

The Electra turned right at Five Points. Hump turned. Now we were three cars back. "Passing Plaza Park," I said. "Staying in the center lane so far."

"Turning onto Peachtree at Five Points," Art said.

"Move up soon as you can," I said. "I don't want him to make me."

"I'm trying."

"At Alabama," I said. "Still in the center lane."

"Got you and the Electra in sight," Art said. "Take a left on Mitchell and a right on Pryor."

I nodded at Hump. "He's yours," I said to Art.

Hump made a left turn onto Mitchell. One block and he took a right onto Pryor. Now we were parallel with the green Electra and Art's unmarked police car.

"Still going straight out," Art said.

"We're getting back on Peachtree," I said.

"It's turned into Whitehall now," Hump said.

"Whitehall then."

Hump took a right and, a block later, a left that put us somewhere behind Art and the Electra. They weren't in sight ahead. Hump hit the accelerator and started bulling his way through the traffic.

"Pulled into a service station. Dropped a kid off. Heading out again."

That figured. The pick-up man had paid the kid a few dollars to drop him off a distance from the *Journal-Constitution* and to pick him up out front a few minutes later.

"Worth worrying about the kid?" Art asked.

"No," I said, "he's day labor."

"Ahead," Hump said.

We'd made a sharp curve and there ahead of us was Art's unmarked police car. "I see you, Art."

"Stewart's coming up. He's turning onto Stewart, heading for Hapeville."

"Time to leapfrog," I said. "I'll pick him up."

"He's yours," Art said.

Ahead of us, Art worked into the right hand lane and pulled off the highway and stopped in front of a package store. Hump took a left and we were on Steward. The green Electra was about a block ahead of us.

"Lay back some," I told Hump.

"I've never done much of this," Hump said, "but isn't this just a bit too easy?"

"Bothers me too," I said. "Either he's simple or the trick's coming."

"Where are you?" Art asked.

"Passing the Salvation Army Officer Training School," I said.

"I'm working my way up," Art said.

"Get closer," I said to Hump.

Hump worked his way closer. Now we were half a block behind the Electra. "Atlanta Tech coming up," Hump said. I passed that to Art over the walkie-talkie.

On the left the fence that surrounded Atlanta Tech appeared. Behind the fence I could see the old airplanes they used in teaching aviation mechanics.

"Shit," Hump said.

I looked ahead. The green Electra slowed and took a left through the entranceway and onto the grounds of Atlanta Tech. Hump said, "We follow?"

"No, go on."

"This the trick?" Hump asked.

"Might be." I turned and looked through the rear window. The Electra was going down the road that curved to the left and circled the area where the old planes were parked. It was slow going because there was a speed bump about every twenty yards or so.

"Art," I said into the walkie-talkie," he's turned in at Atlanta Tech. We've gone past. He's in a box."

"Like shit," Art said. "There's a way out. Joins the expressway back there."

Hump found a driveway, pulled in and made his turn. We reached the entranceway and Hump pulled in and followed the same road the Electra had taken. Only Hump wasn't easing down

THE GOLDEN GIRL AND ALL

for the speed bumps. We seemed to be flying about half the time. I put by hands up and tried to brace the hurt ribs. It didn't do much good. Each time we landed on the other side of a bump I could count each rib.

"Sorry, man," Hump said without taking his eyes off the road.

"Keep going," I said.

After we passed the large parking lot there weren't any more speed bumps. I got the walkie-talkie and called Art. "We're behind Atlanta Tech, looking for the expressway connection."

"Stay with it," Art said. "I'll follow Stewart on out toward Hapeville.

At the rear comer of the parking lot Hump jerked to a stop. To the left a large low building with a flag flying over it, a sign in front: *Georgia Educational Production Center.* "Blind end that way, I think."

Hump swung to his right. A narrow road curved away from the rear of the parking lot and he followed that road. It wasn't far to the expressway. Hump hesitated again. Most of the traffic was heading back toward Atlanta, on the far side of the highway. To the right, heading toward Hapeville, it was almost empty. There was no sign of the Electra in either direction.

"Which way?"

"Toward Hapeville," I said. It was just a feeling, a hunch with nothing to back it up. The pick-up man seemed to know the area. If he was headed for some place in downtown Atlanta there were many ways he could have tried to lose us in the confused and seemingly formless layout of streets. Instead he'd led us down a straight line into southwest Atlanta. Then he'd pulled his trick perhaps just on the outside chance that he was being followed. Perhaps just to make us believe that he'd doubled back.

"I hope you're right," Hump said.

In the long stretch, with the almost empty road ahead of us, we could see for two or three miles. Nothing of the Electra yet. Hump looked in the rear view mirror. "Hope there's no cops around." He stomped on the accelerator. We went straight out for a couple of miles, edging past 90, and I'd about decided that we'd made the wrong choice when Hump said, "There's our boy."

I saw the Electra, about half a mile ahead, slowing down to ease into one of the off ramps. "Close on him," I said. I tried Art on the walkie-talkie and couldn't raise him. I braced myself as Hump skidded into the off ramp and then we were following the abrupt rise of the exit road and I tried the walkie-talkie again. "We've, got him, Art. He took the exit…"

"It must be dumb luck," Art cut in on me. "I camped at the right exit. I've got him, you too."

"He's yours," I said. "We'll peel away."

The Electra took a left and we slowed down behind him and took a right. In the rear window I could see Art's unmarked police car tailing away from us. As soon as we lost them completely, Hump made his turn and we were after them again. We took it slow and easy. It was a rundown, tacky section we passed through, fast food shops, chicken to go, trailer sales, and a scattering of bars. It reminded me of the road leading out to the military reservation at Fort Bragg.

"You just passed me," Art said. "On your left."

He was parked in front of a closed and shuttered snow cone shop. Hump did a tight U and we parked next to him. I got out and kicked gravel over to the passenger door of Art's car. I got in.

"We almost blew it back there," he said.

"Where is he?"

"Across the street. The Electra's around back. Can't see it from here."

It was a bar called the Blue Night Lounge. Even this early in the afternoon there were seven or eight cars parked out front. I checked my watch. Almost one-thirty. It was a little early for drinking. I'd been watching myself for the last couple of months.

"We've got ourselves a bird in the hand," I said.

"I'm bushed," Art said. "You and Hump go pick his feathers."

It was dark in the Blue Night. Maybe that was by plan, to make you forget how early it was, to give you the feeling that it was really evening. It was overheated too and the lounge smelled like simmering old beer. The Blue Night was a few steps up from the bars down around the Fulton County Courthouse, the ones that opened at six or so in the morning. The men scattered along the bar seemed to be skilled labor, electricians, plumbers, or construction workers on their day off or waiting between jobs. Only one man had a tie on and it had irregular stains, soup or tomato juice, down near the wedge end that touched his belt buckle. He was seated near the curve in the bar and as we passed I heard him telling the man on the other side of him about the days when he'd sold tons of structural steel in a single afternoon.

I found two stools at the center of the bar, close to the beer taps. Seated, our backs were to the tables and booths. I didn't want the search to be too obvious so I used the mirror behind the bar. It wasn't hard. He was the only one in the lounge who wasn't at the bar. He was seated alone at a table in the far back corner, drinking coffee. The owner, the manager or just a valued customer? As far as I could tell nobody else was drinking coffee and there wasn't a coffee pot behind the bar.

I nudged Hump. He gave me a short jerk of his head. He'd found him, too. The barman came over and I ordered two short cans of Bud. After the barman brought the beers and left with our money, I said, "We'll give it some time."

"We could just kick his ass," Hump said.

"Not yet," I said. "I think this is probably just half-way there." I looked in the mirror and, as if to back me up, the pick-up man pulled back his shirt cuff and checked his watch. He got up from the table and carried his coffee cup through a door in the rear of the lounge. Hump started to slide off his stool and follow. I stopped him. "Stay easy," I said. "If he leaves Art's out front."

Hump nodded. "Getting shaky," he said.

"That's two of us."

The pick-up man returned a minute or so later with another cup of coffee. He sat in the same chair, the one facing the outside door. He lifted the cup and blew some of the steam away.

That reminded me. I lifted my beer and took a couple of short sips. It didn't taste good this early in the day. It hit my stomach like a large block of ice. I looked at Hump and saw that he was having his troubles as well. "The first one of the day's the best one, right?" I said.

Agreeing, Hump took a large swallow and almost gagged. He gave me an injured look and I could see the muscles in his throat working to hold it down. I waited until it was under control. "It's a busted rope," I said. "He's hired to pick it up. He's to make sure he wasn't followed here. He probably made a call soon as he got here. Said he wasn't tailed. Now, somebody picks it up from him."

"Looked at his watch again," Hump said.

"He's nervous."

The bartender moved down the bar toward us. I said, loud enough for him to hear, "How about seeing if I left that pack of Gold Medal cigars in the car?"

Hump grunted and drank some more beer. "I will in a minute."

The outside door opened and the glare of winter light cut across the bar like a spotlight. Everybody at the bar except Hump and me looked away from the sun. For a short moment a woman was highlighted in the doorway and then she stepped inside and the wind smacked the door closed behind her. My eyes had to adjust to the darkness again but I got a look at her as she passed behind me and angled toward the table in the far back corner. She was a little on the bony side, wearing a tailored pants suit and a woman's tan trench coat over that. The platinum blonde hair or wig was teased up into something like a beehive.

"I'll see about those cigars," Hump said. "Watch my beer."

I pulled his beer close to mine and waited. The blast of wind and light struck again as he went out. I watched the pick-up man and the platinum blonde at the table to see if they paid any attention to Hump's exit. They hadn't. They seemed to be in the middle or an argument. He was shaking his head and she was insisting. Finally, I guess they got it settled and she reached into her shoulder bag and brought out an envelope. He jerked it away from her and held it just under the table top level for his count. She was seated across from him with her legs crossed. Now she was impatient and it set her top leg rocking. It wasn't the slow, steady, auto-erotic leg rock. This was an angry one.

The count must have been right. The pick-up man reached into the breast pocket of his gray suit and brought out an envelope. She grabbed it and stood up, all in one motion. She had a few more words for him and though I wasn't close enough to hear any of them, I could have won a prize guessing some of them.

Hump came in and walked down the bar to his stool. I pushed his beer back to him. "Couldn't find the cigars," he said, "so I guess you left them at the apartment."

"Probably," I said.

Hump lowered his voice. "Art had it figured soon as she drove up."

"What's she driving?"

"Yellow caddy convertible."

The blonde whirled away from the pick-up man. As she passed I turned on my stool and gave her my best bar watcher looking at a girl thing. I got a look at her face this time. I tagged her age around twenty-five. It looked like she'd lived those twenty-five the hard way and nobody was ever going to pick her for under thirty for the rest of her life.

"Art'll follow," Hump said. "He said he'd come back for us as soon as she settles somewhere."

"You mean we've got to drink some more?"

"Seems so," Hump said. "Never heard you complain so much before."

RALPH DENNIS

"It makes sense," I said. I could see, in the mirror, that the pick-up man was still at his table. He was facing the front entrance. "Leaving right after the broad might make him wonder about us. He might make a phone call."

The barman passed and I waved a hand at him. He brought over two more cans of short Bud. I freshened my glass and sipped at it. The barman dropped my change on the bar and said, "I haven't seen you two in here before, have I?"

"Just passing through," I said.

Ten minutes later we left the Blue Night and went out and sat in Hump's car. A few minutes later Art returned. He pulled off the highway and made a u-turn. "Got her planted," he said over the walkie-talkie.

Hump backed out and we followed him past all the neon and the fast food chrome. A couple of miles from the Blue Night he swung off the four lane into a two lane. Not far from the main highway we were in the center of a low rent residential section. Houses on both sides of the street, and perhaps another layer or two of houses behind the ones that fronted on the street. They were a little better than the usual cracker box but not much. The main difference I noticed was that there was some choice about whether the home owner wanted the carport on the left or the right.

The yellow caddy looked out of place in the driveway of 124 Mason Tower Road. The driveway and carport here were on the right side and the lawn was overgrown and wintered yellow.

Art drove past and we tailed him around a turn and parked behind me, out sight of the house and the caddy. Art came back and eased into the back seat.

"You'd better stay out of this at first, Art." I said.

"If you're going to do what I think you are, you might be right," Art said. "The police don't believe in ass-kicking without a warrant."

"I'd like to know who else is in the house. Any men, any shooters."

"There are ways," Art said, "but you always got this hurry-hurry thing going."

"You could find out who the phone is listed to. Might give us something to make a guess on."

'I'll call in." Art got out and went over to his police car.

"I've got a feeling we're going to do something silly," Hump said.

"Like kicking doors open, storming in, things like that?"

"I'd rather not," Hump said. "That's a way of meeting a bullet head on."

"They're checking," Art said when he returned.

"I could use some iron if you've got a spare."

Art opened his jacket and reached back on his hip. He brought out his own, a Smith & Wesson .38 with a two inch barrel.

I dropped it in my topcoat pocket. We were dragging our feet. It was past time and we didn't know how to do it. There wasn't an idea among the three of us. I grabbed the door handle. "Might as well," I said.

A truck with *Ideal Odorless Laundry* on the panels came around the corner. It passed us and parked ahead a couple of houses. A fat black man got out and walked around to the back. He got out a package of laundry and walked across a lawn up to the house. I looked at Hump and grinned and he grinned back.

"Art," I said, "Hump wants to go into the laundry business."

Art was waiting at the truck when the laundry man returned with a bag of dirty clothes over his shoulder. Art showed his I.D. and the black man appeared interested until they talked for a minute or two. He seemed reluctant. I got out and walked over to them. The black was saying, "... couldn't do it without the company saying it was okay."

I held out two twenties and a ten. "Rent for ten minutes," I said.

The laundry man took the bills and said he had nothing against helping the police. No sir, ask anyone and they'd tell you he was a good citizen.

CHAPTER ELEVEN

Hump drove around the block and parked the truck behind the yellow caddy in the driveway. He was wearing the tan jacket with *Ideal Odorless Laundry* on the patch over the left breast pocket. The jacket was too small and he left it unbuttoned on the chance that it might not be too obvious that way.

I was in the back of the truck, seated with my hands clasped over my knees. I could hear the ribs grating with each bounce and it was hard breathing with the pain. Now and then I'd have to reach up and push one of the bundles of laundry aside as it tipped toward me. Over my head, the plastic wrappings of the cleaning swished and cracked.

Hump opened the rear doors and nodded at me. He selected a couple of dresses from the rack above and a bundle of laundry from the stack at my feet. He left the doors open and as soon as he moved away I ducked out of the truck. I kept the truck between the house and me and reached the cab. I took another step and looked over the hood. Hump was at the front door. He struggled to get a hand free. That done, he found the door bell and pressed it. I got Art's .38 out and duck-walked up to the bumper.

The door opened. I couldn't see who it was. Hump helped out. He said, "Laundry and cleaning for you, lady."

That meant it was probably the blonde. She said something I didn't hear. Hump said, "It's no mistake." He looked down at the label on the laundry. "See here. It says 124 Mason Tower Road."

The platinum blonde who'd been at the Blue Night stepped onto the porch. Hump turned his head toward me as the blonde

RALPH DENNIS

edged around and looked down at the laundry label. Hump dropped the laundry and grabbed the woman. One hand covered her mouth. He swung her away from the door. She kicked at him and he stepped aside.

The door was wide-open. I sprinted across the lawn and up the front steps to the porch, gun in hand, at the ready. The living room was empty and I was halfway across it, keeping to the rug, when I heard the man's voice from the open doorway straight ahead. "What is it, Joanie?"

I couldn't answer him. Even if I grunted it wouldn't sound like her. I kept going.

"Joanie?" There was concern in the voice now. "Damn it, Joanie."

We hit the doorway at the same time. He was a hairy bastard wearing nothing but shorts and we grunted with the impact. I swung at him with my left hand and he ducked under it. My left never was any good anyway, so I tried to bring the right up and hit him with a pound or so of S. and W. but his hand closed on my right wrist. He was pushing the gun away and I didn't want to fire. He went into a kind of bunny hug dance. He was trying to shake the gun out of my hand and I was trying to knee him. He kept taking the knee on his thigh and when I tried to kick him he slipped the kicks like he'd had plenty of practice. His weight and strength was getting to me and I was having trouble breathing. He'd hit the bad ribs a couple of times and the last time was a wicked punch that pushed me toward the doorframe. When I was close he put all his strength into it and swung my gun hand against the frame. It felt like I broke a knuckle or two and the gun kicked out of my hand and bounced into the bedroom. He pushed me away and made a dive for the gun. I recovered enough to stagger after him. He got the gun and was turning, swinging the gun up and twisting toward me, when I reached him. I was tired and hurting and I wasn't about to wrestle with him anymore. I took a final stride toward him and kicked him in the mouth.

112

The teeth crunched like gravel underfoot and he forgot the gun and grabbed his mouth. The outside door slammed. I braced one arm across my chest over the ribs and stepped past the man on the floor and got the .38.

Hump came in, holding the blonde by the nape of the neck like you hold a kitten. She was struggling and kicking and spitting. Hump held her up on her tiptoes and looked down at the man on the floor. He wasn't out, but he was dazed. Blood was dribbling out of his mouth and he was spitting out chunks of teeth.

I eased down on the foot of the bed. My breath was a hard roar that came close to deafening me.

Hump looked at me and shook his head sadly. He said something I couldn't hear.

"What?"

He said it louder. "You have to mess him up this much?"

"He wouldn't hold still," I said.

The blonde, Joanie, made a noise somewhere between a gurgle and a scream. Hump released her and she ran over and fell on her knees beside the fallen man. She jerked a corner of the sheet from the bed and started dabbing at his mouth.

"Where's the little girl?" I asked.

"You son of a bitch," Joanie said.

"Where's the little girl?" I repeated.

"What little girl?" she said.

I took a shuddering breath and stood up. "I'm not going to ask it many more times. Where's the kid?"

"I don't know anything about any kid," she shrieked at me.

"This your man here?"

"Yes," she said. "And look what you've done ..."

I cut her off. "Hump, take her out for a minute. I'll talk to him. He'll tell me what I want to know."

"Sure." Hump leaned over and got her by the shoulders and lifted her. She twisted and kicked at him but he laughed and side stepped it and marched her toward the doorway. Hump paused in the doorway and said, with mock concern, "You're not really mad with this guy, are you?"

"The shit I'm not. He busted me in my bad ribs."

The blonde was crying. "Don't hurt him anymore."

"He's all right," I said. "They'll fix his teeth for nothing in the Federal pen."

"In the pen … for what?"

"Kidnapping," I said. "That's a Federal crime, sugar."

"Don't call me sugar," she said.

"Take her out in the yard," I told Hump. I walked over to him and drew back like I was going to kick him about groin high. "He's going to talk to me. If he can't talk he'll write it with a pencil and if we can't find a pencil he'll write it in blood."

Hump didn't move. "You might kill the guy," he said.

"That's his worry. Get her out of here."

I started to bring the shoe forward and she stopped me as I figured she would. "She's in the kitchen closet."

The guy on the floor looked at the blonde and said something to her that sounded, through the wreckage of his mouth, like "You dumb ass."

"Watch them." In the living room I got my bearings, and found the kitchen. They were messy housekeepers and the sink was piled with dishes. The breakfast plates were still on the table with the curdle of grease and specks of eggs.

I yanked the kitchen pantry door open and there she was. Maryann was stretched out on the floor, on a blanket. Her hands and feet were taped and there was a patch of tape over her mouth. She was awake and when she saw me her eyes widened and she wanted to scream. When I reached down for her she kicked out with both feet and caught me on the shin.

"Maryann, it's all right. I'm a friend of your father. I'm taking you back to him."

She was still kicking when I got her up in my arms, but it seemed like reflex. I repeated it to her from close up, whispering in her ear and she went slack in my arms and lay back looking at me.

I put her into a chair at the kitchen table. I peeled the tape from her mouth first and her tongue came out and played across her lips and she sucked in deep breaths. "You thirsty?" I asked.

"Yes, please."

I got her a glass of water at the sink. At the same time I got a paring knife. After she gulped from the glass I put it aside and cut the tape from her hands and from around her ankles. "You want to try to walk?"

"Yes, sir," she said.

She tried but her legs seemed stiff and not willing to carry her weight. I scooped her up and carried her through the living room and outside. I wanted to get her out of that house, out into the cold bright afternoon. The bundle of laundry and the dresses were gone from the porch. Art was standing out at the truck with the driver. He nodded at something the driver said and came over to me. "He wants his jacket back from Hump."

"Maryann," I said, "this is Art and he's a policeman and he has children of his own so you can trust him."

Art smiled. "Hello, Maryann."

Maryann wasn't ready to smile yet. I nodded in the direction of the house. "They're in there. The blonde and her boyfriend. He's got a busted-up mouth. They're both pretty shook right now. I'd like to ask them a few questions but first I'd like to get Maryann somewhere she'd be safe."

"Any ideas?" he asked.

"Marcy," I said. "I'll need Hump's car keys."

"I'll send him out."

Hump came out and handed me the keys. He took the jacket over to the laundry man and shook hands and watched the truck back out. Back at the porch he asked, "You want me to stay here?"

I nodded. "And take this back to Art." I turned Maryann so she couldn't see the gun. I opened my jacket and Hump reached in and snaked the gun from my belt and waistband. He held it behind him as I turned back to face him. "I'll be back as soon as I can."

"What do you want to know from them?" Hump asked.

"Who they're working for or who they're working with," I said.

"Might be on their own."

"Be sure of it."

"Hold Maryann for me a second," I said. He held her while I got out of my topcoat. I wrapped the topcoat around her and she looked at both of us with the same, still frightened face. I guess I didn't blame her at all.

I called Marcy from a pay phone down the road. When I explained it to her she said she'd meet me at the Bek's down the street from her office. She was waiting in a booth when we arrived. She took one look at Maryann and asked, "Would you like to go to the bathroom?"

Maryann nodded shyly. Marcy took her hand and started away from the booth. "Men don't know anything about girls," she said. "Do they?"

I didn't hear Maryann's soft answer but I saw her emphatic us-girls-against-the-world nod and I knew that it was going to be fine between them. When they returned they were chattering away like great friends and I felt out of it altogether. They seemed to be barely tolerating me. So much for me as the hero on the white horse, loved by children and adults. Not that I took it very seriously. I'd have bought King Kong lunch if, after all she'd been through, Maryann seemed to like his company.

With prompting from Marcy, Maryann admitted that she was hungry, just a tiny bit. They went through the menu item by item and still ended up ordering cheeseburgers and French fries and cokes. Bek's doesn't have table service. I stood in line and worked my way through. It took a few minutes and they were giggling like children over something when I unloaded their baskets in front of them. "I like a good joke," I said.

"So do we," Marcy said and they went off in a giggle again.

It was time to leave. I wanted to get back to the house at 124 Mason Tower Road. I pushed my half finished coffee away and stood up. "You'll be at your place?"

"Yes," Marcy said.

"I'll call," I said.

"Are you on expenses this time?"

I said I was.

Marcy held out a hand. "I need some money. Maryann and I are going shopping."

"For what?"

"Underwear and socks and a new dress." Marcy leaned over Maryann. "See how men are?"

Maryann looked at me shyly and said yes.

I held out my roll and Marcy took two twenties. "If it's more you can pay me later," she said.

I decided to play the role she'd given me. "Where does this shopping take place … at the Federal Reserve Bank?"

"Rich's," Marcy said.

"Is it a good store?" Maryann asked.

I left them discussing stores. I guess I was lucky they hadn't decided to shop at Neiman-Marcus out at Lenox Square.

It was quiet in the living room of the house at 124 Mason Tower Road. The guy with the busted mouth had his clothes on now. He was seated on the sofa with a towel pressed to his mouth. The blonde, Joanie, was next to him, legs prim and proper in front of her and arms crossed under her breasts.

Art met me at the door and we walked back to the kitchen. "They've decided they don't know anything. As soon as you left they got their guts back."

"Did it all themselves, huh?"

"Better than that," Art said. "They don't even know how the kid got into the pantry. One minute she wasn't there and the next she was. The blonde says she'd just found her in there and she was about to call the police and report it when you two broke in."

"That's a story for you."

Art reached into my shirt pocket and helped himself to my cigarettes. "All they needed was a little time to think up that simple crap."

"What now?"

"I've called for an ambulance and a cruiser." He looked down at my shoes. "You ought not to wear those steel-reinforced shoes."

"Didn't know I was," I said.

Back in the living room I said to the blonde, "That's a real science fiction you two are telling."

"It's the truth," the blonde said. "What are you holding us for?"

"Kidnapping," I said.

"Who's your witness?" she shrieked at me.

"The kid."

"Who's going to believe a kid like that?"

"A jury," I said. "All she had to do is convince the judge she knows the difference between lying and telling the truth and that she'll tell the truth."

"No death penalty anymore," Art said. "Too bad about that."

"But lots of hard time to do," I said.

The blonde opened her mouth to say something but the guy next to her lowered the towel and showed us the bloody side. It hurt him but he got out something that sounded like, "Shut up, Joanie."

So much for that. I went into the bedroom and found the phone. I dialed Jack Smather's number. The wonder-body girl answered and when I said who I was she connected me with Jack.

"It worked out," I said. "I've got Maryann."

"How is she?"

"She's fine. Call Simpson. As soon as I turn her over to him I'll put in my bill and take myself out of this."

"Where is she?"

"She's with Marcy."

"Who had her?"

"A guy and his girlfriend. Not sure who they are. We're not even sure how they fit into this. Art's not sure what he can hold them on, but he's taking them in. If we can't find anything we'll make up something."

"That's good work," Jack said.

"It was luck," I said.

Hump and I left Art with the couple and started back for Atlanta. We passed the ambulance and the cruiser a couple of blocks away from Mason Tower Road.

Hump dropped me at my house. I called Marcy's apartment first thing. No answer. I looked at my watch. The stores were still open. If it was a real shopping spree, perhaps they'd tried more than one store. It would be, if Marcy saw it that way, an opportunity. After all that had happened to her, it was certainly one way of making her feel like a little girl again. Hell, knowing Marcy, they might have gone to a movie.

I stretched out on the bed for an hour or so. When I got up it was getting dark outside. I wanted a shower but I was carrying too much tape. I settled for a sponge bath and a couple of hand-fuls of after-bath talc. I struggled into clean clothes and tried Marcy's number again. When there wasn't an answer this time either I didn't have any ready-made reasons why Marcy and the child weren't there. It scared me for both of them. I went over to the closet and got down the shoebox I kept my cash in. The .38 P.P. was there on top. I checked the loads and dropped it in my pocket.

It was usually a fifteen minute ride to the apartment complex from my house. I made it under that time by two or three minutes. It was cold and the wind was up now that it was getting dark. Since she'd moved in they finished the rest of the apartments and they'd planted some grass so there wasn't as much clay dust blowing out there.

I parked next to Marcy's car. I wanted to believe maybe they'd just arrived, but I felt the hood of the car passing it and it was ice cold. So much for clutching at impossible things.

No lights in the apartment. I ran the doorbell anyway. I gave the knob a try and found it locked. I rounded the apartment at a run and found the kitchen entrance in the lowering dark. The back door was cracked and I slammed the door open. There was the smell of burning and I found a sauce pan on the stove, burnt dry over a gas flame. Hardly stopping I cut off the gas and lunged through the kitchen door into the living room. Nothing in the living room. I went on and found her in the bedroom. She was kneeling on the floor, her upper body on the bed. Her back was to me and she was shaking and sobbing and trying to dial a number on the phone. I reached her and turned her. Her lower lip was swelling and there was some blood on her chin. High on her right cheekbone there was a bruise about the size of a man's fist.

"Jim, I've been trying to call you."

I lifted her and helped her stretch out on the bed. I cut on a light in the bathroom and wet a hand towel. "Tell me about it, Marcy."

"Two men ... I didn't see them really ... both very big ... were in the apartment ... they were waiting. One grabbed Maryann and she screamed ... I tried to stop them ... and one of them hit me ... I don't know how many times."

I washed away the blood and the tears. "Both men were big men?"

"Big as you," she said.

"How long ago?"

"I don't know. I blacked out ... fainted, I guess. What time is it now?"

I didn't need to check my watch. "Around seven."

"We got home about five. We'd had a good time shopping and…"

"Easy," I said.

"Jim…I'm sorry…that poor little girl…she was just beginning to feel she could trust me…and then I let them…"

"Not your fault," I said. "It's mine."

I rinsed out the hand towel in the bathroom sink and then went into the kitchen and put some ice cubes in it. Marcy was staring up at the light and crying and I put the towel of cubes against her cheek and told her to hold it there.

I dialed Hump's number. His angry burn came up to match mine in no time at all. He and Marcy were good friends. I guess a part of that, though we'd never talked about it, must have been his feelings about my sometimes desolate life. And I think he saw inside Marcy well enough to understand those after-thirty nightmares an unmarried woman has. Especially a southern woman.

"Is she all right?"

"I think so." I reached over and moved the cluster of ice cubes down Marcy's face to the swollen lip.

"Two studs, huh?"

"Yes," I said, "but if they were the same two one of them has grown a few inches."

"That kid must feel like a handball," he said.

"I can't leave here right now. Drop by the Crystal and find the guy who's reading Hip magazine. I need another meeting with Peggy Holt."

"And if I can't set it up?"

"Feel around. Keep the lie up that we've got Maryann. See how they react to that. Do they seem to know better? Things like that."

"You'll be at Marcy's?"

"Yes."

"Call you back," he said.

"I don't understand this," Marcy said, after I put the phone aside.

"I'm not sure I do either. There's Harper. He's freelance, probably working for himself. The couple we got the child from. Not sure but I think they're hired help. Given time maybe Art can find out who they're covering for. I don't see either of them with the guts to kill Harper."

"What happened to the letter?" Marcy asked.

"I don't know." It hadn't seemed important at the time and I wasn't sure that it was now. It lost its importance as soon as we had the child. "Why?"

"It's a loose end."

"There are always loose ends," I said. It would be easy enough to find out. A call to Art would settle it. I'd been putting off any kind of call to Art. It wasn't going to make him happy that we'd blown a half day's work. "You really want to know, Marcy?"

She shrugged and covered half her face with the wadded towel of ice cubes.

I dialed Art at the department. He listened me out, holding the outburst until I'd finished talking.

"Jesus, Jim, can't you do anything right?"

"You want to come say that to Marcy's fat lip and bruises?"

"No." He softened it. "She all right?"

"Yes, but she'd like to know what happened to the letter we followed from the *Journal-Constitution* building."

"It wasn't on them when we searched them," he said.

"Ideas?"

"One. Probably made a call, read the letter over the phone. Tore the letter up, burned it, flushed it, something like that."

"Before we got there," I said.

"There was time."

I said Hump and I were still working.

"Great," Art said, "call me in about a week and tell me how you're doing."

"You serious?"

"I need the sleep," he said.

Hump called at quarter to eight. "No trouble. She seems to want to meet with you. The same place you talked the other night. Nine on the dot."

"Any reaction?"

"You know the one we talked to at the Crystal the other night? The one who didn't even know anybody named Peggy Holt? They all seem that way, don't show anything."

"Where are you now?"

"A phone booth near Eighth and Peachtree," he said.

"Come over to Marcy's. I don't want to leave her alone."

"Be there in fifteen," he said.

At night you couldn't see much of the damage that the ice storm a week and a half back had done. Crossing the old bridge at the west end of the park my headlights played across a tree that had been uprooted and had fallen against the embankment. The top half had been cut away to clear the approach to the bridge. The rest of it remained.

I parked on the Brookridge Drive side of the park. Down in its center Orme Park was pitch black in shadows. The outer edges were lit by the street lights and the overflow cast by porch lights. I sat in the car and watched for a few minutes. An old man entered the park from the other side and came down the long flight of steps. I didn't get a good look at him but I could tell he was old by the way he moved, the stiffness in the hip joints, the cautious downward movement. He got lost in the shadows but I found him again when he lit a cigarette. From the location, the flare of the match, I guess that he'd taken a seat in the double swing to the left of the steps.

Ten of nine. A young girl bundled in a heavy coat and scarf came down the street from the direction of Amsterdam. She was walking a huge Dalmatian. Under one of the street lights I got a good look at her. It wasn't Peggy Holt. This one was a girl in her teens. They went into the area by the bridge and the Dalmatian romped and the girl called to him, her young voice hanging in the wind like a leaf. The voice thin and weightless. At five of nine the romp ended. The girl and the Dalmatian went over the slight incline and onto Brookridge Drive. I watched them into the shadows, moving toward Amsterdam.

I got out and walked to the double swing that Peggy Holt and I had shared the night before. I lit a cigarette and felt the cold slats warm under me and I swung a little back and forth, waiting. I wasn't sure she'd be on time. She was getting foxy, careful. Being on the run did that to you. Not trusting anybody. Afraid to believe, afraid of strangers and friends alike. Not sure but that your weaknesses would betray you. Careful of your strengths too, because those could be used against you.

Nine o'clock. I flipped the cigarette away and stood up. I stretched and tried to get the heat flowing. Then, as my arms came down, I caught movement in the corner of my left eye. At the footbridge that crossed the narrow stream. I settled into the double swing and put my hand into my right hand coat pocket, felt the butt of my gun, and angled the coat so that the barrel pointed toward the footbridge.

As he moved out of the shadows I saw that it was the old man. He paused at the water fountain and sucked up a mouthful, then twisted to the side and spat it out. He saw me when he turned away from the fountain. He walked toward me, that same stiff, jolting walk. He was a few feet away from me, in more light now, when I decided that he didn't belong in Orme Park anymore than I did. He looked like one of the winos from down on Whitehall or Mitchell. The clothes that had been slept in, the glint of stubble beard. Even closer the fuzz on what must have been a castoff overcoat. He stopped and grinned at me and the grin showed the gap where the five or six front upper teeth were missing.

It amused me. I was about to be spare-changed a few minutes after nine at night in Orme Park. If not that, it was going to cost me a few smokes to get rid of him. I didn't want Peggy to find me with someone. It might blow the whole thing. They might not wait to see that the one with me was a wine-head. I took my hand off the butt of the .38 and stood up. I reached under the topcoat into my trouser pocket and felt for some change.

"You Hardman?" the old man asked.

"Why?"

"Let's go to your car," he said.

"Why?"

"She sent me for you," he said.

The directions he gave me didn't make much sense. First we went completely around Orme Park a couple of times and then he pointed me toward Los Angeles at the east end of the park and we followed that until it touched on Highland. At Highland we made a right and crossed Virginia. A couple of blocks down Highland, before we reached Ponce De Leon, he had me pull into the parking lot in front of the Superior Food Store. He reached over and cut the headlights.

The whole time he'd been watching the traffic behind us.

"I came alone," I said.

"Had to be sure," he said.

"If you're sure, where now?"

"The parking lot at Arlen's."

"Now?"

"Now," he said.

Aden's, the big discount store, had closed down most of its operation a few months back. All that remained was the food store. It was open twenty-four hours a day. The parking lot spread out for what appeared to be acres and acres. It was empty now except for thirty or forty cars bunched near the entrance to the food store. The old man pointed me toward the cluster of cars.

"What now?"

"Park," he said.

I eased into a spot on the edge and cut the ignition and the lights. I got out my smokes and lit one. "We wait, huh?"

"I'll take one of those," he said.

I lit one for him and put my head back and relaxed. It had been a long day and it wasn't over yet.

I think I almost dozed. What shook me out of it was the old man's sudden movement on the other side of me. He opened the door and slid off the seat. He stepped aside and a girl got in and pulled the door closed behind her. I blinked at first, but I put it together without stuttering. It was Peggy Holt, now in a blonde wig. Or she'd cut her hair and bleached it.

"We talk here or drive around?"

"Talk here," she said. "Did you get Maryann?"

I told it one more time. I was getting tired of admitting how I'd blown it. Next time I'd send telegrams. Or singing messengers.

"That was a royal fuck-up," she said at the end of it.

"The people who want what you have increase by the day," I said.

"It was Raymond the whole time."

"You sure of that?" I could check on Raymond. It wouldn't be fun. I knew him because Hump and I did a dope run to New York now and then for him. It was living and eating money.

"It has to be."

"Proof?"

"No," she said impatiently, "but who else could it be?"

"It's not his style," I said.

"Whose side are you on?"

"Not yours. Not your husband's. Nobody's." I paused. "That's not true. I'm on Maryann's side."

"How was she?"

"Getting over the crap the last time I saw her. Scared to death again I guess. My girl got beat up because I thought Maryann needed somebody around who wouldn't frighten her with muscles and man talk."

"I'm sorry about your girl... what's her name?"

"Marcy."

"I'm sorry about that." She faced straight ahead and took a long breath and let it out slowly. "Now I think we'll have to pay the stuff to get her back."

"The others agree to that?"

"Not all of them, not yet anyway. But they will. It'll be hard because it's so much money. More than any of us have ever seen before."

"How much stuff?"

"More than two pounds," she said.

"How much more?"

"It's close to three."

"And your deal... what you suggested in your letter?"

"Half of it for Maryann," she said.

Three pounds. That was a stunner. I'd been thinking in terms of a lot less. A half pound or a pound. It was hard to figure the street value exactly. It depended upon how it was cut. But I could figure their part of it, before the other middle men got involved, at least three to four hundred thousand.

"That's a lot to give up," I said. "And Randy's dead now and the pipe's gone dry."

"Yes."

"How'll you hear if they accept the deal?"

She shook her head. "It won't be in the newspapers. It'll be another way."

"How?"

She slid a few inches toward me. Close enough so that the scent of her got into my skin. "You've tried to help, Hardman, and I appreciate it even if you weren't trying to do it for my sake."

It was a good scene. I clawed at myself to keep my distance.

"But now," she continued, "we're going to buy her back. I want you to quit now, for Maryann's sake. You can't help and you can get in the way. I don't want anything to happen to her. I don't know you well but the way you talk you must want her safe too."

"You want it that way? Me out of it?"

"Yes." She reached behind her and fumbled for the door handle. She found it and pushed the door open. She was turning, sliding across the seat when I stopped her.

"Getting Maryann back doesn't close it out. Randy King's dead and the police won't drop it. They'll keep coming until they've found you. After that it's a matter of how much they want to burn you."

"I won't be in town that long," she said.

I drove straight from Arlen's parking lot to the Schooner Bar on West Peachtree. The Schooner was Raymond's front, his legit business. It covered him like a security blanket. He bought his city and state licenses and paid his taxes and he gave to charities like any Chamber of Commerce member. He kept straight books and he kept the whores and the pimps out of his place. As far as I know there'd never been a disturbance at the Schooner he hadn't handled himself.

The sign out front reached to the edge of the sidewalk. It was a kind of two masted schooner with neon rigging that kept changing colors while the outline of the ship remained steady, the same blue neon.

The sign sputtered at me as I ducked under it and went inside. I pointed toward the inside room of the bar when Fred Epps, a bartender I knew, moved down the bar toward me. He nodded and waved and I went through the doorway and into the nautical setting. Captain's chairs at the tables, netting all around, ship models on the tables, and paintings of ships on the walls.

THE GOLDEN GIRL AND ALL

I skirted a stage where a stripper was working and almost made it to Raymond's office before one of the waitresses caught up with me. "Raymond in?" I asked.

"He's not seeing anybody right now."

"He'll see me. Tell him Jim Hardman wants to see him."

She was gone less than a minute. She waved me toward the doorway that had *Dancers Lounge* on it. I pushed through the door and found myself in a small room. There were a few chairs peppered around the room and a table with a deck of greasy cards dealt for a hand nobody was playing. There was a sofa too, along the wall to the right. A girl in a g-string and a narrow bra was stretched out on the sofa with a towel over her face. She didn't move as I crossed the room and went through the doorway to the left. There was a bathroom to the right on the hall and straight ahead a closed door with nothing on it. I knocked on the door.

"Come in."

Raymond was seated behind the desk. He was a small man, very sleek, very neat. His size bothered him. He wore elevator shoes and he was still shorter than he wanted to be.

There were two large ledgers on the desk and he marked his place by putting one open ledger face down on the other one. He nodded me toward a chair. "What can I do for you, Jim? As I told you over the phone there's no need for a run to New York right now."

I didn't take the chair. Any way I did it, it wasn't going to be easy. I knew Raymond well enough to know that he wouldn't let it be. Small talk wouldn't change it. I jumped right into the middle of it.

"It's something else. Two guys worked me over last night. This afternoon late somebody worked my girl over. I have trouble believing this but somebody's been trying to tell me the wrecking crews come from you."

"Why would I want to rough you?"

"It's a long story," I said.

He accepted that. A man's business was his own. "I can cut this short. I didn't send anybody after you."

"Your word?"

"My word." He met my eyes straight and level.

"You kidnap any six-year-old girls lately?"

He wasn't that good an actor. It flew right past him. "You been drinking or something, Jim?"

"Or something," I said.

"I'll say it one more time. I didn't rough you or your girl and I never did a kidnap in my life."

"Sorry," I said.

"I'll take it this time." The hard edge, the blood edge was in his voice. "This time. Never again."

"I needed to know. It narrows the field."

Raymond looked past me. "Close the door behind you, Mr. Hardman."

I did. I closed it so there was hardly a sound. And let a shuddering breath out.

CHAPTER TWELVE

Hump left the bedroom door cracked and tiptoed across the rug toward me. "Marcy's still sleeping."

"What did Janice say?"

Hump looked at the roast beef sandwich I was eating. "Any left?"

"Plenty," I said.

"Janice said she'd take a cab and be here in ten minutes." He went into the kitchen and came back with a huge chunk of beef and one slice of bread wrapped around it. "You know all those girls of mine jump when I ask a favor of them."

"I was afraid she might be busy."

"Waiting for my call," Hump said. "What else?"

"What else?" I grinned at him.

"We going somewhere?"

"Like good citizens we're going to see the police. That's the first stop."

"They way they love you there, that'll be a short visit," Hump said. "You've got my curiosity up. What do we do after that?"

"Maybe we kick ass," I said.

"If this doesn't check out," Art said, "I'm in big, big trouble and you know it."

"If it doesn't check out I'm going to die of surprise and a heart attack," I said.

We were deep in the guts of the building, going down a long windowless tunnel that led to the Records and Evidence Storeroom. It was going toward midnight and Art had had to work his way up through channels. As reluctant as he'd been I was surprised at how hard he pushed for it. How he argued and raised hell and said that it was important if they were going to break the Randy King killing wide open. In the end that was the argument that overcame the hesitation at each level.

And yet, I felt some strong regrets that Art had to be the one to do the pushing. It wasn't going to do his career any good. It would hurt him. Cops were clannish and however it worked out they weren't going to like him for turning the rock over.

I knew that nothing I'd said could push him anywhere he didn't want to go. He was, at heart, just a damned good cop and he wanted to know what the truth was. Once he knew, the department could do their own clean-up or cover-up. Hump and I had agreed to that. No matter what the result we'd swallow it and choke it down and let the department handle it any way they wanted to.

So there we were, making a hell of a racket in a deserted tunnel. Art and Hump and me and two young cops from the narcotics squad. Art insisted on that. Two men to do the check who weren't from his division.

It was inventory day. Unannounced.

The uniformed cop behind the desk in the Records and Evidence Storeroom did what he was supposed to under the circumstances. He called the watch captain upstairs and talked to him. He said, "Yes, sir" a couple of times and then he hung up. He then got his inventory clipboard and the ring of keys. He handed them to Art without another word.

Within half an hour the pattern was clear enough. Art and Hump and I stood aside and let the two young cops do their work. First they'd gone through the inventory sheets and they'd blue penciled all the items of evidence that included hard drugs.

After that it was a matter of going through the numbered wired-in cages. They'd weigh the contents and check it against the inventory and then taste a fingertip of the powder. Right away, with the first ounce, I heard the whisper, "Talc."

And later, after they'd checked out eight or ten, I heard one say, "They must have bought all the talc in Atlanta."

"An ounce here, an ounce and a quarter here … it adds up."

"Got careless here or hurried," one said another time. "Took out an ounce and replaced it with an ounce and a half."

"Closer to two ounces," the other said.

Art watched it, not blinking as it added up, but I could read him well enough to know it was making him sick. I almost think he wanted me to be wrong for the sake of the department.

The two young cops didn't talk to us. Without their help I could see it shaping up. The hits and pieces as I kept a running count on my fingers, already added up to at least a pound. And there were still a lot of blue pencil marks to go.

Art walked over and whispered to one of the young cops. He whispered back. Art nodded. He told them to go ahead with their check. When they finished they were to bring the results up to his office. Not to anyone else. Just to him.

On the way back to the front desk Art leaned toward me. "Better than a pound missing already."

"Sorry to be right," I said.

"Recent too," Art said. "The last couple of months. When the story broke about all that heroin being missing from the evidence storeroom in New York … what was it, three hundred pounds? … a check was made down here. It was all here then."

"Who made the check?"

"A team from outside," Art said.

"No way they could cover themselves? Nobody from the storeroom helped with the inventory?"

"They were the ones we were checking on," Art said, shaking his head.

The young cop at the front desk looked at us but he didn't say anything. Art started past him and then thought better of it. "How long have you been on this detail?"

"Am I under investigation?"

"Not that I know of," Art said.

"About a month."

"Did you know Randy King?"

"I knew him. He was on the day shift, the busy one."

"How many on that crew?" Art asked.

"Three. Randy and Bo Turnage and Ed Winters."

"They close friends?"

"I don't know how you mean that," the young cop said.

"Sure you do," Art said. "Did they pal around after working hours?"

The young cop nodded. "They were thick as…" He broke that off and shook his head. "They went to ball games together, drank at the same places."

"What kind of guys are Turnage and Winters?" I asked.

The cop looked at Art, wanting to know if he had to answer my question. Art nodded at him.

"They lived over their heads, I think?"

"How?"

"Well, I can't prove it," the cop said.

"We're not taking your statement right now," Art said.

"You know … clothes, cars, the places they drank and ate …"

"You got any idea where the money for all that comes from?" Art twisted around and hooked a cigarette from my shirt pocket.

"Favors, I heard," the young cop said.

"What kind of favors?"

"Just favors," he said.

"They had to explain it somehow," I said. "It's a good cover. Almost any cop wants to can make a bit off favors."

I stepped around Art. "Turnage and Winters … what kind of size on them?"

"Turnage's a big guy, shoulders like a barn door. Winters' the other way. We used to joke that he probably stood on his tiptoes to make the minimum height."

"That's a knot for me," I said. "And I've got the ribs to prove it."

Art leaned over the young cop's desk and mashed out the cigarette. "What kind of car you drive?"

"A '67 VW."

Art nodded. "Go slow with favors. Some balls are getting broken around here tonight."

We were in the tunnel headed for the elevators. There was a turn ahead and I heard them before I saw anyone. It was a noise I remembered from the stairs outside the garage apartment on Fifteenth. "Company," I said. Art walked on, getting a pace or two in front.

Bear Hodge and Ben King rounded the turn and headed on the straight away for us Bear was pacing himself, trying to lay back with Ben. It was hard on him. He had burn on you could read from a distance of fifty yards. On Bear's right Ben was moving as well as he could under the circumstances. The tile floor didn't give him good traction for the crutch tips.

When Bear couldn't stand it anymore he touched Ben on the shoulder and came at us at a run. Art got another step in front of Hump and me and put his chin out where Bear could reach it.

"What the fuck are these two doing in here?"

"Interested taxpayers," Art said:

"I'm going to have your ass for this," Bear said.

"You mean next month or right now?" Art said. "You can have it now if you want it."

Ben King reached them while Bear was trying to decide whether he wanted it to break that way. He was shaking and sweating from the exertion. He got a hand on Bear's shoulder and pulled him a step away from Art.

"What's this I heard?" Ben asked Art.

"Where'd you hear it?"

"A friend called me," Ben said.

"Who?"

"It doesn't matter," Ben said.

"It matters," Art said. "You see, you're just an interested tax-payer, too."

Ben backed away a few steps and leaned against the tunnel wall. Bear went over to him and asked if he was all right. Ben said he was, that he'd be fine as soon as he got his breath.

Bear looked past Art at me. "This wild hair your idea, Hardman?"

I didn't have to answer. "It's not so wild," Art said. "It's not finished yet, but it looks bad."

"How bad?"

"Over a pound of the hard stuff so far. It might go as high as three or four. Jim here thinks a bit over three pounds."

"God damn it, how?"

"Copycat of the New York thing. Substituted talc for the stuff."

Ben King grunted with effort as he elbowed his way from the wall. "You got some reason to tie this to Randy?"

It was a hard one for Art to handle. I waited to see how he'd deal with it. He did it the only way he could. "I wish I could say we didn't. I think he was, Ben, but we won't be sure until we talk to the other two on his shift. I'm putting out a pick-up order on Turnage and Winters soon as I get back upstairs."

"You're slipping my question," Ben said.

"All right. It's hearsay and circumstantial so far. An informer tells me Peggy Holt has three pounds of hard dope she's about ready to deal. Word is she didn't get it through the usual pipe-lines. She says Randy furnished it to her. Add to that the fact Randy was living with her and it looks bad."

"The pig," Ben said.

It broke the rest of his back, the one that had nothing to do with spinal cords and motor impulses. It smashed the guts and the balls that he'd drawn on to hold the brittle parts of himself together. I was watching his face and I think he knew as soon as he heard it. Maybe he knew even before that. He might have tried to believe otherwise but he knew Randy for what he was, he knew the weaknesses in him. Whatever it was that allowed Peggy Holt to squeeze his balls and lead him anywhere she wanted him to go.

If we'd have been alone I believe I'd have tried to make Ben understand that Peggy Holt had that way with men. She could have made Billy Sunday take up drink and sin again if she wanted him to. That kind of thing. But we weren't alone and there wasn't any way I could say those things to him in front of Bear and Art.

"After you talk to Turnage and Winters," Ben said, "you let me know."

"It's kind of late," Art said. "I'll call you tomorrow."

"Tonight's our poker night. Bear and I'll be playing until sunrise if it takes that long."

"I'll come by," Art said.

Hump and I stepped past Bear and headed for the elevators. Art was a step behind us. I guess Bear wasn't through with us yet. He yelled after us, his voice hollow in the tunnel. "And get those two out of the building. You hear me, Art?"

I waited until the echo died out. "Don't throw me in that briar patch," I said. "I'm leaving anyway."

Art followed us out to the parking lot. It was in the twenties, bitter cold and dropping. It wasn't a night to be out on the streets. It was a night to be home in bed with a warm woman.

Hump got behind the wheel and started the engine. I got on the passenger side and Art got in the back seat. The air coming out of the heater felt like air conditioning.

"Bad back there," I said.

"Yeah."

"The cop in the Evidence room almost said thick as thieves," I said. "Like he'd made a guess before tonight."

"It's the first law. Don't inform, cover up for the other cop."

I pulled up my topcoat collar and fitted it around my neck. "It's in the open now. No reason to cover anything now. Find Turnage and Winters and break them wide open. Hang their guts out to dry."

"Cruisers on the way to their apartments now."

"When you break them I think you'll find that the three of them worked it out together, with some help from Peggy Holt. And somewhere along the way they fell out. Might have been Peggy Holt's doing. Maybe she convinced Randy the pie was better if they didn't cut it as many ways. All Randy and Peggy had to do was play stay-away until the sale was made. Remember what Ben said? Randy was taking some leave. Bet you'll find he and Peggy made a move and tried to get lost. Set up house-keeping and Peggy went up and stole her kid. That probably means they were going to unload the dope and bug out of town. Peggy didn't want to leave without her kid."

"And Turnage and Winters … what could they do … take it to court?"

"They traced Randy to the garage apartment. Had their face-off with him. He told them to fuck off. They were out. Think you'll find they came prepared. Didn't want to use their own iron. Got some lady's pistol from the Evidence room, one that hadn't been used, just confiscated. When they'd taken all they wanted off Randy, killed him and looked for the dope. It wasn't there. Might even have put the lady's gun back on the shelf. What better place to hide a murder gun?"

"So, no sign of the dope. Needed a lever on Peggy."

"That's where Maryann came in. Only Harper got there first." I put my hands to the heater vents. It was getting warm at last.

"So they kill Harper, take the child, want the dope as ransom."

"Only we get the kid before they can make the deal," I said.

"Most of it's speculation," Art said.

"The main thread's there. Some details might change."

"We find Turnage and Winters and we'll find the kid," Art said.

"I thought so too. Now I'm not sure. Can't figure any way Turnage and Winters could have known Marcy had Maryann. That's been bothering me all day."

"Who has her then?"

"I hate to say it out loud," I said. "I want to be wrong this time."

"Whisper it to me then."

I shook my head.

"Looks like I'll be in all evening." Art got out and closed the door.

A couple of blocks away Hump stopped at a pay phone. I got out and checked an address.

CHAPTER THIRTEEN

I stood in the doorway and waited. Hump was behind me and to my right with his hand on the door bell. As soon as the door opened and Jack Smathers was there I reached back, feeling the ribs the whole way and not giving a damn, and hit him with all the strength I had left. His nose broke under it and he fell back and cat down on his rump.

I followed him in and Hump closed the door behind us and locked it. When Jack got over the stunned feeling he looked up at me. "You crazy or something?"

"Not a bit," I said.

Hump leaned down and grabbed him by his jacket front, lifted him and threw him in the general direction of the sofa. "Play time's over," Hump said. "This *is* for real."

Jack landed on the arm of the sofa and rolled into a seat. One hand covered his nose, exploring it. He brought his hand away and stared at the first blood.

"It happened too fast," I said. "That's what bothered me. Given some more time, a few more hours, anybody might have found the kid. I knew and Hump knew and Art knew and we didn't tell anybody. That leaves you. I made a phone call to you. Why not? I was working for you."

"That's crazy," Jack said.

"Say something else," Hump said. "I'm getting tired of that."

"Your wife in?" I walked past him and looked into the bedroom of the apartment.

"She's visiting her mother in Dalton," Jack said.

The linen on the bed looked newly changed, the pillows starched and the sheet and blanket turned down partly on one side. "When's the divorce?"

"It's a visit." Jack worked a handkerchief out of his hip pocket and pressed it to his nose. "I think you broke it."

"When did you start selling us out? I know the why. Peggy Holt, superwoman in bed. Couldn't wait to go trotting back to her with your fly open."

"Say something," Hump said.

"I like money as well as anybody else," Jack said.

"That's not it," Hump said. "It's bedroom tricks you like." Hump turned to me. "Jim, next time you get a chance, you got to introduce me to this Peggy woman."

"First chance," I said, grinning at him.

"You won't get close to her," Jack said.

"Not the way I hear it," Hump said. "Was talking to this black dude at the Crystal this evening. Seems, from what he said, she thinks black is better."

"And the Wildwood Connector," I said. "He's black and used to do her."

"I wouldn't worry about it," Hump said, false comforting him. "It won't wear out and it don't change colors."

"You been selling us out all along or just today?" I asked.

He didn't answer right away. He was pushing it around from compartment to compartment, trying to see if there was some story he could get away with telling. None of them panned out well, I guess. "Today," he said.

"Had this ball ache and saw a way of easing it, huh?"

"Yes." He lowered the handkerchief and felt the bone in his nose. He grimaced at the pain. "You did break it."

"Where's the kid?" This from Hump as he leaned over the coffee table and shook a cigarette from a pack there.

"I don't know. With Peggy, I guess."

"Where's Peggy?" I asked.

"I don't know."

I nodded at Hump. "Take a look in the bedroom and tell me what you think."

Hump stood in the bedroom doorway and started chuckling. "Shit, man, that's a love nest."

"Bet there's champagne in the refrig, too," I said. I gave it a second to level out. "When was she due, Jack?"

He didn't like it. "Two hours ... or three hours ago."

"When you answered the door you thought it was her?"

"Yes."

"Man, you are innocent." Hump put back his head and hooted. When it became a low, throaty wheeze he said, "That cunt's got all she wants and none of that is you. She's got dope worth three or four hundred thousand and she's got her kid and you're so far out in left field you don't even know what happened to you."

"I bet you didn't even get your wick dipped once this time," I said.

"That right, Jack?" Hump said.

He didn't answer. He didn't have to.

"How'd you get in touch with her?" I eased into a chair at the end of the sofa.

"She called me last night. After she talked to you. She wanted to know if you could be trusted."

"Maybe I should have asked her if you could be trusted," I said.

"People like you two, you can't understand. I just couldn't help myself. I heard her voice and I couldn't ..."

I didn't want to hear it. I could make it up. "So she asked if I could be trusted. What else?"

"She said she wanted Maryann back."

"That figures."

"She said she'd do anything to get the kid back," Jack said. "She was crying."

"I'll bet. So, then, she set up the sell out?"

"Yes."

"She give you a way of getting in touch with her?" Hump said.

"After you called me I called the Union Mission and told a man I wanted to talk to Peggy. She called me a few minutes later."

"His name?"

"Frank Benson."

Union Mission. The old guy, almost toothless, in the Park a few hours before. The one who'd directed me to the meet with her in the Arlen's parking lot. Might be him.

"And that's all?"

Jack nodded.

I got up. Hump moved over to the outside door. He unlocked it and waited. "Last words for you, Jack. I'd beat the shit out of you if I thought it'd do any good. I don't think it would. All I'm going to ask is that you get on the other side of the street when you see me coming. Or you dive in a doorway and stay there."

"I couldn't help it, Jim, I really couldn't."

"That's what all the cripples say."

Hump drove back toward the center of town. We stayed on Peachtree until we reached Ellis. He turned left and we could see the huge sign over the old brick building. *Atlanta Union Mission.* It was a place, where for fifty or seventy-five cents a night, the winos and the derelicts could get a bed and a shower. Passing it several times and watching the winos out front getting some sun, I'd wondered how long the Mission would last. It was only a block or so off Peachtree. Too valuable, I thought, for the property to be used that way much longer.

I pointed Hump toward the raised parking lot at the side of the Mission. Hump parked and went around to the main entrance to see if Benson was in. He knew me but he didn't know Hump. It would be Hump's job, if Benson was in, to con him into coming outside. I'd take over after that.

Hump returned alone a few minutes later. "He's not in and they don't know where he is or when he'll be back."

"Might be a long wait," I said. I looked at my watch. One-thirty. The bars were open for another two and a half hours.

"A cold one too," Hump said.

"If the liquor stores were open I'd pop for a bottle."

"Is that all holding us back?" Hump pushed the door open and got out. "I know a bell captain at the Inn down the street. Scalps pint bottles for big prices. After hours, of course."

I got out my roll. It was getting thin. I peeled off a twenty.

Hump hesitated before taking it. "Are we still doing expenses? I'm not even sure who we're working for anymore."

"I'm not either," I said, passing him the bill. "Simpson up in Chapel Hill, I guess."

"Cognac for you, scotch for me."

"Don't be long. If this Benson starts running you'll have to chase him. I'm wore down below the nub."

"Ribs bad?"

"I think they'd be better barbecued." I said.

Assuming Frank Benson was the old man in the park, he didn't show while Hump was gone. Now and then one or two'd come stumbling down the street from one direction or the other. The usual ritual was to finish off the dregs before they went inside. Peach wine or Thunderbird or whatever. Maybe they weren't allowed to bring bottles in the Mission. At any rate they'd gulp down the last of their bottle, prop the empty against the side of the building or drop it in the gutter, and straight-backed as they could they'd march into the Mission.

Winter must be a bad time for a wino. In the spring and summer there were doorways and abandoned cars and empty buildings where they could sleep. That meant fifty or seventy-five cents more for wine or beer. But beer and wine wasn't much good when the temperature dropped under thirty. And tonight it was in the twenties.

THE GOLDEN GIRL AND ALL

Hump dipped his head and got back in the car. He passed me a half pint flask of Hennessey. I broke the seal and got the cap off. I rolled a swallow of it around on my tongue. Burn and sting and God, it felt good burning its track down into my stomach. Relaxing while I waited for the warmth to spread.

"Someday," I said to Hump, "we're going to take a trip to Europe and rent us a house right next to a cognac distillery."

"Scotland for me," Hump said.

"Six months in France, six in Scotland."

"Deal," Hump said. He lowered the pint of scotch and wiped his mouth with the back of his hand. He looked past me, through the side window. "One coming now. He'll be under the street light in a second."

I capped my flask and turned. The street light was on the corner, a distance away, and he was only in the full glare of it for a short time. It was enough. It was the old guy from Orme Park. He had a good load going and the drinks had him talking to himself. His arms were out wide, gesturing, and then he was past the light and in the shadows.

"That's the one," I said.

"Hold my scotch," Hump said. "I brought some bait with me." He reached into his topcoat pocket and brought out a pint of peach wine. "The bell captain, Billy, thought I was going bad or something."

I watched as Hump turned up the collar of his topcoat. He broke the seal on the pint of peach wine and poured about a third of it on the ground. He walked to the front corner of the building and stopped there, partly in the shadow and partly out. He waited until Frank Benson began his cut across the street toward the Mission. Then Hump lifted the bottle and let a bit of the peach wine trickle down his throat. After the scotch the wine must have tasted like pancake syrup.

Benson's angle placed him near the corner of the building where Hump was. As soon as he touched the sidewalk, Hump

lifted the bottle again and took another slug. When he lowered the
bottle he must have said something to Benson. Benson stopped
and came over to him. I guess Hump was offering him a drink
because the old guy nodded and reached out his hand. Hump put
the bottle in his hand and turned him and eased him into the
darkness at the side of the building. They were only a few yards
away from the car. Benson lifted the bottle to his mouth and Hump
put a friendly hand on his shoulder. Then the hand wasn't friendly
and Benson let out a squawk and dropped the bottle. It shattered.
Half-lifting, half-pushing, Hump brought Frank Benson over to
the car. I reached back and opened the back door. Hump rammed
Benson in head first and slipped into the seat next to him.

I slid over behind the wheel and started the car. I backed out
of the lot. Behind me Benson said, "If this is a robbery…"

"No robbery," Hump said.

"If it ain't a robbery…"

Benson must have kicked out or swung at Hump. I looked up
in the rearview mirror and saw that Hump had him by the back
of the neck, shaking him. "Easy or I'll break it," Hump said. "And
it won't be much of a chore."

"You want something from me?" Benson asked.

"Some words," I said.

I could see he was leaning forward, trying to get a look at me.
Maybe he thought he remembered my voice. "Do I know you?"

"We met in a park," I said.

"Hardman?"

"That's the one," I said. "The one who's going to break your
neck is Hump Evans."

"You wouldn't do that," Benson said.

"Of course I'm not," I said. "Hump's going to do it for me."

"Whenever the man says do it, I'll do it," Hump said. He
reached out his arm and I put the scotch where he could reach it.
He held the bottle between his knees and got the cap off with his

free hand. "Like I'd wring a chicken's neck," he added before he lifted the bottle and had a drink.

"You helped con me tonight," I said. "I don't like being conned. I don't like it at all. Hurts my reputation. First thing you know people'll start thinking they can con me anytime they want to. They'll laugh behind my back. That's why you're good as dead right now. That's why they're going to find you in the morning with a very funny looking neck."

He was beginning to buy it. But he had to try one more time to see if he couldn't talk himself out of the corner. "I've heard about you, Hardman. They say you're straight. Killing me wouldn't be your style." He put as much front on it as he could. "And that's why you're not going to kill me."

"You're not listening, Benson. I didn't say I was going to kill you. Hump's doing it for me. He owes me a favor."

Benson believed it now. "I think I can make this straight with you, Hardman. Nothing's so bad we can't talk it out."

"You've been staying on at too many prayer meetings after you ate the soup," I said.

"No, I mean it."

"I think he means it," Hump said.

"You backing out on me, Hump?" I made it hard and nasty. "If this is the way you pay back a favor ..."

"You know me better than that," Hump said. He sounded like his feelings were hurt.

"You said you wanted some words," Benson said.

"That was before I changed my mind," I said.

"You want to know how to find the girl, Peggy. That's right, ain't it?"

"I don't need your help finding her." We reached the split in Peachtree, where it divided into Peachtree NE and Peachtree NW. I took the northwest fork. "They're building a new wing on Crawford Long Hospital. That's a good place to dump him."

"Everybody's trying to find her and I'm the only one knows where she is," Benson said.

"Construction site's always good," Hump said.

"Is it a deal," Benson asked, "is it?"

"You already conned me once today. Why should I believe you this time?"

"I give my word."

Hump laughed. "He's a stand-up comic too."

"Is it a deal?"

"Tell me and I'll see if it's worth anything," I said.

"A deal, right?" He was beginning to freak out because I reached Crawford Long and made my turn that would take us by the side of the new wing under construction that faced Peachtree NE.

"We'll see," I said.

"I'm going to take your word," Benson said. "We've got a deal so I'm going to trust you to keep your part of it." He sucked in a deep breath. "You'd never find her in a million years. Nobody'd find her."

"That's enough whipped cream." I pulled to a stop beside the construction.

"She's in Underground Atlanta," he said quickly.

"Hanging around down there?" Hump said.

"She's living there. You know where the tracks go through?"

"I know the place," Hump said.

"Across the tracks hasn't been built up much. No shops or bars yet. One black tried and went broke over there. Started a soul food kitchen. Called it Aunt Edna's Soul Food Kitchen."

"Got it," Hump said.

"She's living there, in the boarded up restaurant. Her and her little girl and the guys who work with her."

"How many guys?" I asked.

"Two when I left there a while ago. Sometimes there's more."

I pulled away from the curb and turned onto Peachtree NE, heading back downtown.

"I knew you'd keep your word," Benson said.

"For tonight," Hump said. "If you lied to us we'll be back."

"Tell him what we want him to do," I said.

"We're going to drop you at the Mission. You go to bed, pull the covers over your head. Don't go out and don't make any phone calls.

"I swear it," Benson said.

We rode in silence the rest of the way. I stopped across the street from the Mission and Hump opened the door for him. "Remember," he said.

Benson bobbed his head and said, "Yes, I swear" and then he scooted across the street and into the Mission. I waited a minute and when he didn't come back out I headed for the closest entrance to Underground Atlanta.

CHAPTER FOURTEEN

Before and after the Civil War the main thing that Atlanta relied upon was its importance as a railroad center. It caused one big problem. It got so that people couldn't get from one side of the tracks to shops on the other side. Overpasses were built. In time these overpasses were extended until the tracks were below the streets. While this made crossing downtown streets easier, it stranded, below the streets with the tracks, dozens of shops and warehouses.

For years these shops and warehouses were boarded up, abandoned and almost forgotten. Until a group of men formed an association and began encouraging others to open bars and restaurants and shops down there where the main business district of Atlanta had once been. The food ran from French to Middle-Eastern. In the shops a tourist could buy a box of candy or a mink coat. Or a red-necked t-shirt from the Lt. Governor's shop and get it autographed for another seventy-five cents.

It was, I always thought, something of a tourist rip-off place. The prices were geared for expense accounts and throw-it-away vacation money. And lately, there seemed to be gangs of young hoods hanging around the entrances, waiting to roll a drunk or rip off a cash register from one of the small shops. That's crime in Atlanta. Can't do much about it.

I parked in the lot at the corner of Alabama and Pryor. Hump and I ducked through the narrow entrance and followed the ramp until it leveled out. It was going toward closing time, the crowd thinning, and I guess it had been a bad night. In front of the Crepes de Paris a girl was handing out copies of the menu and price list. I could count the goose pimples on her bare legs.

We went straight through. It wasn't a long walk. We reached the stairs that led down to the tracks. There wasn't much light across there but enough so that we could see the boarded-up front of Aunt Edna's Soul Food Kitchen. To the right of the Kitchen there was a wide walkway, angling down, that ran up to the streets, the parking lots up there. To the left we could see the dark fronting of as yet undeveloped property.

"That's it," Hump said.

"Looks likely," I said.

"Doesn't it, though?"

I stepped away from the railing. "I'm going to call Art."

"While you do that ..."

"Yeah?"

"I'll check the back, the street side, for ways in and out."

I watched him start across the tracks. Then, feeling the urgency, I went looking for a pay phone.

I didn't see Hump anywhere. I'd been gone about ten minutes and that should have been time enough for his scout around.

"Here," Hump said behind me. He handed me a hot dog and a cup of coffee. "You reach Art?"

"Should be here in ten minutes or so." I took a bite of the hot dog and guessed it was one-fourth meat and three-fourths cereal. I washed it down with the coffee. "What's it like over there?"

"Confusing," Hump said. He motioned across the tracks. "What we're facing is really the back door. Oh, I guess when the kitchen was open you could enter from this side. But the real entrance is up there, on the street. Big glass windows and a big doorway."

"What's confusing?"

"I don't see how they'd get in and out. This entrance and the one up there on the street … they're boarded up tight. No way out unless they've found a way to get through boards."

I pointed over toward the undeveloped area to the left of the Kitchen. "Might be some connection between the Kitchen and the blank front over there."

"Maybe." He finished his hot dog and drank the rest of his coffee. He looked around for a trash can. Not finding any, he wadded the hot dog wrapper and put it in the cup and threw them over the side, down to the tracks. "I'll give it a look."

I waited at the railing. This time Hump angled to the left, bypassing the Kitchen fronting. After he was beyond the tracks he stepped up onto a narrow walkway. He put out a hand and ran it over the wall, moving slowly to my left as he did it.

I checked my watch. Still some time before Art would arrive. When I'd talked to him he'd seemed eager to rush right over. The search for Turnage and Winters had drawn a blank. Neither had been at their apartments and now it looked like the questioning might have to wait until they showed up for the regular shift in the morning. Even that was "iffy." There was always the chance the word had gotten to them about the inventory. If it had they'd probably headed for tall cover. Art would probably get to them sooner or later, but I knew how much Art disliked the chance that it would be later.

Across the tracks Hump turned and made the gesture of turning a door knob and pushing a door open. So there was, after all, some kind of door in the fronting even if it didn't show from a distance.

It would be a step ahead, knowing that, when Art arrived with his raiding party. In our talk he'd said he send one car to cover the other side of the Kitchen and he'd come in the way I had and meet me at the railing beside the track. I looked in that direction. Still no sign of Art. It was getting close to time.

THE GOLDEN GIRL AND ALL

When I turned back to look across the tracks toward Hump I got my first sense of it getting away from us. The two men, I first thought, were a couple of tourists coming down for a last couple of drinks. And, as they came out of the walkway and into the light, I got a prickling, a warning. One of the men was big, hulking, and the other slim, very slight. The two cops gone bad, Turnage and Winters. Then, as if to make it certain, they didn't cross the tracks. Instead, they did a sharp right and stepped up onto the narrow walkway.

They weren't looking in my direction. I was shouting it under my breath, look over here, Hump, but he had his back to me, exploring the door frame. He didn't look around. There wasn't anything I could do without blowing the whole operation wide open. If I yelled I'd warn Hump but I'd also warn the two rogue cops. Except for the fact that Hump was right in the middle of it, all of our eggs were very obligingly getting into the same basket. We couldn't have planned it better. So I said, under my breath, sorry about that, Hump, and watched helplessly while Turnage and Winters walked right up on Hump and took him.

I didn't see a gun but I assumed there was one from the way Hump let it happen. He was cool, knowing I was across the tracks and Art was on the way. Otherwise, he might have made a try. He stood very still while the big man frisked him.

I put my back to the tracks and walked away. I knew they might look across the tracks. If they did I wanted them to see the back of some heavy-set tourist who was on his way to another bar before closing time. At the same time I wasn't just walking away. I was looking. I settled upon a young couple. They seemed sober and they didn't seem in any hurry. I tagged them as being in their twenties. He looked like he'd dressed for a big night and she, wigged and badly made up, was overdressed too.

"You want to make a quick ten dollars?" It wasn't a good opening, but I didn't have much time.

It offended him. "What do you mean...?" The girl swung away and edged behind him.

"Police business," I said.

"Well..." He looked back at his girl.

I got out the ten and put it in his hand. "Stand over by the stairs. In a minute or two three or four cops are going to get here. Ask if one of them is Art Maloney."

"Art Maloney," he repeated after me.

"Tell him the two cops he's looking for are already over there and they've got Hump. And I've gone over there."

"The two cops he's looking for... they've got Hump... and you've gone over there."

I took each of them by an arm and turned them. "Walk to the railing with me. We're laughing. We're having fun."

"Yes, sir," he said.

I laughed and he laughed and the girl added a shrill giggle. When it died out I leaned on the railing and looked across the tracks. I didn't see Turnage and Winters or Hump. That meant they'd gone into the Kitchen by the door Hump had found. "See the boarded-up front of the Soul Food Kitchen? Now, thirty or forty feet to the left, there's an indentation. That's where the door is."

"I see it. Yes, sir."

"And for god's sake," I said, "stay here until the police show up."

"We will," he said. His girl nodded.

"Do this and I'll treat you to the best dinner in Underground." I patted him on the shoulder and went down the stairs. I crossed the tracks at a fast jog. At the walkway, stepping up, I looked back at the young couple. They were still at the railing. I just hoped they wouldn't decide I was a practical joker who was setting them up on a snipe hunt.

I found the door without any trouble. There wasn't a knob or a handle and I might have had some difficulty except for the fact that it was ajar, cracked an inch or so. I eased it open another

THE GOLDEN GIRL AND ALL

inch and put my eye to the opening. Nothing. Pitch dark. I didn't
hear anything either and that bothered me. It could mean they
were waiting for me. Not likely, I told myself. Hump wouldn't tell
them so there wasn't any way for them to know I'd be coming
after them.

It was a good argument. A very good argument. But it didn't
make me want to step into the darkness beyond the door. What
made me go, trying to find the balls for it somewhere, was that
I was worried about Hump and I wanted to help Maryann. The
rest of them could go to hell in a laundry cart.

I took a deep breath to ease my breathing after the jogging
and let it out in short hisses. I swung the door open just wide
enough for me to slide in sideways. I stepped through and pulled
the door almost closed behind me, all in one motion. As soon as
I released the door I stepped to the side and waited. I stood with
my back to the wall, waiting for my eyes to get used to the darkness. I could make out just the big shapes at first. It seemed to be
a storeroom of some kind. As time passed I realized that I was in
what had been at one time part of the restaurant. The big shapes
were tables with chairs stacked on top. Ahead and to my right I
could see a thin pencil line of light. Probably a doorway. Light
leaking from within. I pushed away from the wall and headed
for the doorway. I took it one step at a time. I could see the tables
and the stacked chairs but I didn't know what might be on the
aisle floors. That way, it took quite a bit of time to reach the pencil
line of light. Even before I reached it I began to hear the almost
inaudible rumble of voices. The lows from Turnage or Winters
and the highs from Peggy Holt.

I reached the doorway. It was wider than I'd thought. A
swinging double door. The narrow line of light was coming from
the center, where the doors met. I put my eye to the opening. I
could only see a narrow slice of the room beyond. I saw part of a
black man and beyond him one of the cops with a .38 lined up.

"And if I don't?" Peggy asked.

"I'm going to kill that big black bastard over there. Just so you'll see what dying's like."

"Then?" Peggy said.

"The little black there and then on down the line until just you and the kid are left."

I put up a hand and felt the top of the door. It was, as I thought, glassed. Someone had very carefully covered the glass half with newsprint. It was a workmanlike job, no cracks or spaces. I got out my pen knife and cut a small triangle in the newsprint. With that done I could see into the room. It was a large boxy space. To the rear of the room there were a couple of what looked like army surplus double bunks. Closer to me, almost centered in the room, they'd pushed a couple of the tables together. I could see the remains of a late supper they'd been eating when Turnage and Winters had surprised them.

To my right, just within the sightlines, I could see Peggy Holt. She was seated at the end of the table. Next to her, looking sleepy and puzzled, was Maryann. She was on Peggy's right, facing the door. One black was on the near side of the table, his back to me. He didn't have his hat on but I guessed that he was the young black who'd delivered the letter to the *Journal-Constitution* building. Beyond him, standing up with one hand on the top of a double bunk bed, was the big cop. He had the .38 and he was playing it around the room.

The rest of the room. There was another black on my left, seated at the other end of the table facing Peggy. I'd never seen him before. He was older, gray peppering his hair. Beyond him Hump was standing with his hands clasped behind his neck. The small cop was next to him. He was holding a .45 automatic that looked too big for him.

"We want the whole thing," the small cop said.

"Half," Peggy said. "That was, the original deal."

"That was before you talked Randy into getting foxy with us."

"It's not fair," Peggy said.

"Sorry about that," the slim cop said. The big cop laughed, dry and cutting.

Take him up on it, I was saying to myself. Get him out here in this dark room.

"Half," Peggy said.

"You must think we're kidding. Is that what you think?"

"I don't think you're going to shoot anybody," Peggy said.

"You've been living here long enough to know that trains still passed through here, right? We checked and one'll be passing through in nine or ten minutes. It's a long, long train."

Peggy looked down the table at the older black. He nodded. That meant the information about the trains was accurate enough.

"When the train passes I start killing. Make up your mind."

"All right," Peggy said. "Bobby, you take him to the one and a half pound cache."

The black with his back to me nodded.

"All of it," the big cop said, "or no deal."

"Half or no deal," Peggy said.

The two cops looked at each other and I saw them agree to go along with it. It didn't mean that they'd given up on the other pound and a half. That wasn't likely. They'd take half now and then see if they couldn't work something with the rest of it later.

"Okay," the small cop said. "Half's better than nothing."

"Isn't it though?" Peggy said.

"Freddie," the small cop said, "you go with him and come right back when you've got it."

"Sure," the big cop said. "Glad to." He pushed away from the bunk bed and rounded the table. He put a hand on the young black's shoulder. "Let's get at it."

It was time. It was going to break one way or the other and I hoped that Hump hadn't let himself go to sleep. I thought I could handle the big cop. Surprise would help in that. I wasn't sure I wanted to go up against the .45 the small cop had. Hump was going to have to chip in on that problem. Heads up, dammit.

I got out my .38 P.P. and flattened myself against the wall. No matter which way the door opened, in or out, I didn't want them to get a glimpse of me. Less chance of that if the doors opened outward, toward me.

Luck was with me. The young black pushed at the door and it swung out, covering me. The black passed me and I could smell the sweat on him. Right behind him, gun out, the big cop stepped through the doorway and let the door close behind him. His eyes were on the black in front of him and as soon as he'd taken one step past me I moved in behind him and put my .38 in his spine. He froze.

"Easy," I whispered. "Drop the gun hand to your side slowly."

He was doing that and I was reaching up to take it from his hand when the young black, Bobby, suddenly realized what was happening. At first I think he just turned to see where the big cop was and then he saw the two of us. One look was enough. He swung around and made a run for the outside door. One arm struck a stacked chair and it fell to the floor with a loud clatter. I looked up and the big cop took my hesitation in taking the gun from him and used it against me. He swung the gun back up, away from me, and kicked back at my shins.

In the lighted room the other cop was yelling. "Freddie, what's going on out there?"

"Somebody's out…"

I drew back my left and hit the big cop in the kidney as hard as I could. That turned the rest of what he was saying into something like a scream. He was crumpling forward. I reached in one more time and tried to hit him with the gun butt. He slipped that and even as he was falling he was trying to bring the gun around toward me.

I said, "Shit," and fired down at his legs. I think I hit him in a leg or a foot and the gun he'd been turning toward me flew out of his hand and bounced across the room.

The door banged open behind me and light cut a wide rectangle across the room, ending just under my feet. I turned and I was bringing up the .38 as fast as I could but I knew I was going to be late. The cop had the .45 up and out and I wasn't lined up yet. I braced myself. Wherever he hit me it was going to be like getting kicked by a mule.

After that, maybe I could get a shot in. Maybe not.

CHAPTER FIFTEEN

"You." He was squeezing the butt, taking that safety off, ready to put one right between my eyes. I was still trying to get my .38 up but at the same time I was figuring the angle. It was going to make my nose look funny, if I had any nose left.

Hump flew through the doorway and hit him about neck high. He got off a round but it went wide, into the far wall, and then Hump separated him from the .45. It fell to the floor. Then, grunting, Hump nudged him with a shoulder and the small cop spun across the aisle and rammed into a table and a group of chairs. He bounced back and that was one more mistake. Hump stepped toward him and hit him with about a six inch punch. The cop went down and twitched at Hump's feet.

I'd taken my eyes off the big cop. My back was to him. Now, he'd moved behind me and swung a huge hand at me. It wasn't well aimed for his purposes. It hit me in the ribs on my left side and I went down. I could hear him running away, limping or dragging one foot. I looked up and Hump had picked up the .45 from the floor. He was fumbling with it and then the door opened and closed behind him.

"Let him go," I said. "Art's probably outside."

Hump leaned over me and helped me to my feet. "Watch the group in there."

I staggered toward the outside door and kicked it open. I stepped outside into what looked like dress-inspection day down at the department. Six uniformed cops were lined up on the tracks facing the door. I lowered my gun and walked out slowly.

To my left the young black, Bobby, was spread-eagled against the wall, a riot gun on him while he was taking a frisk. The big cop, the one I'd pinked, was being rammed against the wall by two of the biggest cops I'd ever seen. He was trying to tell him he had a hurt foot but they just weren't listening.

Out front, gun at the pistol range stance, Art stood shaking his head at me. I walked over to Art and handed him my .38. The few paces over to him the riot guns traced me. They relaxed only when Art took my gun.

"I want it back," I said.

"We'll see." He pocketed it. "You all right?"

"Fine," I said. I looked across the tracks and saw the young couple there, leaning over the rail. They'd been joined by about fifty tourists. I grinned at them and waved. The girl waved back. "I'm fine," I said again for no reason at all. "But you better tell your men to get their asses off this track. There's a train due in a minute or two."

I leaned against the wall and watched them brought out. They'd backed a paddy wagon down the walkway and they were loading them in roughly, with no ceremony at all. The last one out was Peggy Holt.

In the grim light down there she wasn't any Helen of Troy. She needed a bath and the blonde wig wasn't on quite straight. I could see a few dark hairs had worked their way out from under.

"You win some and you lose some," she said to me as she passed.

"It was time you lost," I said.

"Fuck you, Hardman."

"Not you, sugar, not the best day you ever had."

I stepped away from her and went looking for Maryann. I found her sitting on one of Hump's broad shoulders. She looked down at me solemnly. "Where's Marcy?"

"Waiting for you," I said, "and your friend, Hump, is going to take you to her."

"Where'll you be?" Hump asked.

I dug out the car keys. "Making that visit with Art."

He shook his head at me. "You don't need that grief."

"Tonight or a year from now, it'll still be there."

I turned and walked out with them. I stayed on the narrow walk and watched them cross the tracks and go up the steps to Underground Atlanta. Art walked over to me.

"The young couple," I said.

"The ones by the steps?"

"Yeah, I owe them the best dinner in Underground."

"They left." He reached in his topcoat pocket and brought out a scrap of paper. "I got his address."

I took the scrap of paper and put it in my pocket without reading it. "I hurt all over."

"You need a drink." He took my elbow and turned me toward the walkway up to the street "We might get offered one."

"Who else?" I asked.

"Who else, what?"

"Who else plays with Bear and Ben King?"

"Nobody," he said.

"Nobody?"

"They play two-handed."

I shook my head at that. Two handed, like old maids. It was damned sad and lonely and maybe it was just because I was tired and hurting, but I felt a knife cut of pain. I think I got a feeling of what the death and now the shame of Randy meant to Ben. It was another door that had turned into a wall and now there weren't, except for Bear, anymore doors left.

"I told him it was silly and foolish," Bear said. "He's too damned hard-headed for his own good."

Bear was talking in a whisper and he wouldn't look at me. He was angry enough with me to take me out in the parking lot and work me over. The way I felt he wouldn't even break a sweat doing it.

Ben was in the bathroom. He'd been there when we'd arrived and he hadn't come out yet. Bear had let us in and he'd kept us standing. Though there was half a bottle of Jack Daniels in the center of the poker table, he hadn't offered us a drink.

It was a small apartment, an efficiency. We were in the tiny living room that was almost crowded out by the poker table. Straight ahead I could see the kitchen-dining room. To the right was the bedroom and beyond that the bathroom.

"It's not altogether my idea ..." I began.

"Leave then," Bear said.

The john flushed, the pipes creaking and Bear threw up his hands and walked away. The door opened beyond the bedroom. He must have been walking on the rug. I didn't hear the tap-tap or the slide of his shoes at first. He looked about the same as he had when we'd seen him earlier. But now he seemed so worn down that he couldn't make it from the bedroom doorway to the poker table. Ben didn't argue this time when Bear met him and gave him a shoulder and helped him into his chair.

"Art, Jim," he said when he got his breath, "how about a drink and a hand of poker?"

"One hand," Art said. "Jim's banged up and I've got to get back to shop and wrap this one up. Or start wrapping it up. It might take days."

"Daniels all right?"

"Rocks," I said and Art nodded.

Ben motioned me into a chair directly across from him. Art took the chair on my right. He gathered up the cards and ran them through a good hard shuffle and passed them to Ben. Ben held the cards and waited until Bear returned from the kitchen with two old fashioned glasses with ice in them. He handed me the glasses and the bottle and I poured for Art and me.

"Jacks or better," Ben said.

"What game?" Art asked.

"The only one. Five card draw."

"Fine with me," I said.

"Nickel, dime, quarter."

I got out a couple of ones. Bear made me change from a cigar box. Art fumbled and brought out a five. Bear gave him three ones and the rest in change.

"Ante," Ben said. He threw in a quarter.

"Pot's right," Bear said.

Ben dealt the cards. He couldn't make it all the way across the table. Bear followed each card, pushing it toward the right player. When all the cards were out I picked up mine. I'd made a good start. I had three deuces, a four and a queen.

"So it's over?" Ben said. He hadn't looked at his cards yet.

"Almost," Art said. "As soon as we get the dope back."

"You talk to Turnage and Winters yet?"

"A little." Art spread his cards and looked down at them. "It looks like Hardman had it figured right. The three of them were in it together from the start. Peggy Holt must have convinced him to double-cross the other two."

I noticed that Art hadn't used Randy's name. Not once.

"It's by me," Bear said, turning to me.

I threw in a dime. "Open."

Art followed and added his dime. Ben took his time over his cards, as if trying to decide if they were worth the trouble of playing them. Finally, with a disgusted shake of his head, he tossed in two nickels.

"The thing," Ben said, "is to play nickel, dime, quarter just like you'd play for dollars." He smiled at Bear. "Bear hasn't learned that yet."

"Three cards," Bear said.

I got my two cards and left them face down on the table, watching Art and Ben. Art drew three and Ben drew two. That was interesting, if you could believe Ben's statement about playing it like it was for real cash.

"Why'd he do it?" Ben asked.

"Money," Art said, "and the girl …"

"No," Ben said, "I want to know what Jim thinks."

"It'll be a guess," I said.

Ben nodded, the thick folds of flesh shaking.

I lifted my first card. An eight of spades. No help.

"Something's happened. I don't know what it is. There's no core to anything anymore. No center. Honesty used to be its own reason. The love of one good woman used to be enough."

I turned my other card. A queen. That made the argument for keeping a high kicker.

"And it's not anymore," Ben said.

I shook my head. "You can't blame Randy really. It's the time, the way things are. It looks like our heroes are sort of super-pimps, guys who fuck and rip-off as many women as they can. No heart, all cock. Kids look at the rich and they see how money can put you above justice. That makes money more than a thing to buy groceries and beer with."

I tapped my cards back together and waited. I thought of the three cards Ben had kept. Might be a pair and a kicker.

"Go on," Ben said.

"So here's Randy. All wrapped up in one package, he's got the money-chance and the golden crotch. It was what the times told him he wanted and he went after it."

"This girl, Peggy Holt, could she have gotten to you, Hardman?"

"Maybe," I said. "Maybe not. If I was Randy's age, it's likely. Right now if some golden girl fifteen years younger than I am acts like I've got the only cock in town I reach back and check my wallet."

Ben grinned at that. "How about Art?"

"Same answer," I said. "Unless it happened to be a time when a good Catholic like Art needed a little sin to spice his life."

"Are we going to play cards?" Bear demanded.

Ben and I kicked it back and forth. Bear and Art dropped out. I ended up spreading my three deuces in the center of the table. The long look at his cards and my thought about the kicker had suckered me. He beat my deuces with three tens.

"You believe that talk back there?" Art asked.

"Partly," I said.

"Which part?"

We were a block or two from Marcy's apartment complex and we'd been silent until now.

"Which part?" Art insisted.

"All of it," I said, "except that Randy was probably a greedy little animal who deserved what he got."

"Why didn't you say that back there?"

"No percentage," I said.

I stood over Marcy's bed. A night light in the corner of the room gave enough light so that I could see that the bruise on her cheek was darkening. But she was in a deep sleep. The sleep that comes after pain and fear and tension.

Next to her, curled up and bent to shape herself to Marcy's back, Maryann looked like a happy child. It would take her a few days to get over the crap of the last few nights. Maybe it would take longer, but right now she seemed fine.

I stood there for a long time. Marcy's hair was blonde and Maryann's was black but they might have been mother and child.

After a time, I went back through the living room into the kitchen and had another drink. After that drink and another I kicked off my shoes and slept on the sofa in my clothes. I didn't have strength enough to take them off myself.

AFTERWORD

The Literary Life of Ralph Dennis

by Richard A Moore

R alph Dennis (1932-1988) was born in South Carolina and had a master's degree from the University of North Carolina, where he also taught. For mystery fans, Dennis will always be associated with the City of Atlanta, the locale for the twelve novel series about Jim Hardman, former cop and unofficial private eye, all published by Popular Library between 1974 and 1977.

Seldom has a city played such an important role in a series as Dennis delighted in sprinkling his novels with the restaurants, bars, nightclubs, hotels and street corners of his adopted home. I don't know when Dennis moved to Atlanta but I can vouch for how well he knew the city for I spent most of the 1970s as a reporter in that city. And I admit that I derive special pleasure from the splendid depiction of a city I lived, worked and played hard in for that decade.

The decade was nearly over and I had become a mystery writer myself before I ever read a word by Dennis. The late Jud Sapp, bibliographer of Rex Stout, shoved a copy of the fourth novel in the series, *Pimp For The Dead*, into my hands and said I had to read it. Jud was an elementary school principal, and looked it, so given the title and the packaging, the recommendation was more than a little incongruous. From the first few pages, Dennis had me hooked and I've remained a fan.

The Jim Hardman series was packaged similarly to all the other action heroes of the time—the Destroyer, the Executioner, the Lone Wolf, and on and on. Each novel had a number as well as a title in these series because that helped the fans keep track of which they had read. The plots of so many of these series were too interchangeable for a reader to keep track without the aid of a numbered system.

The Hardman series was trumpeted as "A great new private eye for the shockproof '70s," which was funny, since Jim Hardman was far from the typical action-adventure hero in other numbered series. He was middle-aged and as out-of-shape as most guys who get their primary exercise lifting beers or glasses of J&B Scotch. And he lifted quite a few.

Hardman had more than his share of fights in the novels, with mixed results. The true muscle was provided by Hardman's friend Hump Evans, formerly a defensive end with the Cleveland Browns. Today having an Afro-American sidekick who provides the muscle or does the dirty work is something of a cliché—it wasn't in the 1970s. More importantly, Hump was always an equal partner with Hardman. Hardman didn't shy away from brawls; it was just that Hump was better at it. At 6-6 (or 6-7 as both were given at different times) and 270 pounds, Hump always retained a certain independence from Hardman. There was nothing demeaning about Hump or his relationship with Hardman.

The Dennis publishing history is interesting. The first Hardman novel appeared in April 1974 and a total of seven Hardman novels were published in that first year.

It was not unusual for a publisher to have three novels in a series ready to go out simultaneously or in quick succession in order to establish the concept of the series with the public. This was done with John D. MacDonald's Travis McGee, for example. But seven novels in one year was very unusual for a series that was not being ghosted.

Here is the publishing sequence of the first seven Hardman novels:

Atlanta Deathwatch April 1974
The Charleston Knife is Back In Town May 1974
The Golden Girl & All May 1974
Pimp For The Dead June 1974
Down Among The Jocks July 1974
Murder's Not An Odd Job August 1974
Working For The Man September 1974

That is an incredible record of productivity. The Hardman novels do show signs of hasty construction at times but given this publishing schedule, it is amazing that Dennis could maintain the quality at this pace.

The eighth Hardman did not appear until 1976. In the intervening two years, Dennis published two novels, *Atlanta* (Popular Library 1975) and *Dead Man's Game* (Berkley January 1976), then returned to Jim Hardman with the eighth through twelfth books in the series. Here's is the publishing sequence for the final batch of Hardman books:

The Deadly Cotton Heart November 1976
The One-Dollar Rip-Off January 1977
Hump's First Case March 1977
The Last Of The Armageddon Wars May 1977
The Buy Back Blues July 1977

Dennis finally achieved a hardback sale with *MacTaggart's War* (Holt 1979). By far his most ambitious work, the plot concerns an attempt to hijack the gold bullion that Britain moved to Canada for safekeeping during the dark days of World War II. While not completely successful, this novel outshines so many others that made the bestseller lists and were grabbed by Hollywood. At the time of publication, Dennis must have felt himself on the brink of a breakthrough. *MacTaggart's War* was a great read and it would have made a wonderful Clint

Eastwood movie. Alas, this was the last Dennis novel to be published.

I moved to Washington in 1981 but made trips twice-a-year to Atlanta. Oxford Books was always one of the places I visited, especially after they opened an Oxford II that featured used books. One day as I looked around Oxford II, I noticed this bald, middle-aged guy at a counter going through the new arrivals and pricing them. It was Ralph Dennis. I recognized him from a newspaper picture some years before.

We chatted for several minutes. I wondered why I had not seen anything by him in several years. He pointed to a Richard Stark novel about the tough crook Parker that I had in my pile. Dennis said he had written a novel with a lead character that made Parker look like a sissy. His editor was enthusiastic and Dennis thought it was his best work. Unfortunately, the editor was let go by the publisher and his replacement did not care at all for the novel. It was the old story of the orphaned novel and writer. A publisher intended to reprint all the Hardman novels and oddly started with the second *The Charleston Knife's Back In Town* (alas, the reprinting did not extend to the others as planned: it just wasn't to be).

All of this took place as other store personnel buzzed about us with censoring looks. I felt guilty for taking up his time and perhaps getting him in trouble as other staff members had hovered near us during our conversation.

Some months later I went back and he wasn't there. At the cash register there was a Ralph Dennis memorial sign and I was shocked to learn of his death.

Time passed and some years later an evening came when I was drinking and thinking and I picked up the phone and put my old reporter instincts to work. I tracked down Ralph's sister Irma in a town where she owned and ran a restaurant and asked her about Dennis. She told me that she'd loved her brother. As his situation and his health deteriorated, she'd begged him to come live with her. She'd felt she owed him that much because he had meant so much to her growing up. He refused out of pride and he died not long after. There was a memorial held in his honor at his favorite Atlanta bar, George's Deli.

Some years later, I reconnected with his sister and we had many cheerful conversations and she filled me in more on his background. Ralph earned an MFA from the Yale School of Drama and he was well on his way to a doctorate when he had a falling out with his faculty advisor and dropped out.

His playwriting ambition continued in North Carolina and two of his plays were produced in Winston-Salem. He also wrote fiction but nothing sold. He moved to Atlanta in 1970 and it was there he wrote the first Hardman novel, which quickly sold. The Hardman series provided a living, and he had a comfortable life, but he was restless for bigger things.

Irma visited him in Atlanta, where he lived in the Virginia Highlands neighborhood within an easy walk of his favorite bar. He had a favorite booth where, after a day of writing, he could sip beer, watch people and hold court.

I wish Irma and I had talked more about their difficult childhood. I know that she was the oldest of three children, followed Ralph and William, and that they ended up in an orphanage when their father died in South Carolina in 1941.

According to the records I've found, the kids left the orphanage at some point and in 1945 were in Jacksonville Beach, FL where Ralph and William went to school and Irma supported them as a waitress. In 1946, they were back in South Carolina, where Irma worked as a cashier in the Dixie Double Dip Ice Cream Cup while her brothers continued in school. Somehow, they got through it together.

Irma and I very much wanted to see Ralph's work back in print. I was excited to learn that she had copies of several of Ralph's unpublished novels. She sent them to me to read and they were longer, more ambitious work that what Ralph had done before. But there was also one shorter book, entitled simply *Kane,* and I knew after reading just a few pages that this was the novel Ralph told me about in our only meeting—the one that was "orphaned" when his editor left and his new editor hated the book.

Kane was a intended as a sequel to his 1976 novel *Dead Man's Game* (which is very difficult to find now) and featured a hitman who was indeed extremely hardboiled and ruthless enough to rival Westlake's Parker. The *Kane* manuscript had the new editor's comments scribbled all over it... and it was clear that he didn't understand the character or the genre at all.

I desperately wanted to see Ralph's work get back into print, but there wasn't much interest. There was one nibble from a publisher in 2004, but then Irma died and the rights to Ralph's worked passed on to her heirs.

In the many years since then, interest in Ralph's books has remained high among paperback collectors and crime novel writers, but no publishers came calling until 2014... when Lee Goldberg tracked me down and asked for my help locating the heirs and securing the rights.

Now Lee's publishing company Brash Books, which he founded with Joel Goldman, is bringing back all of Ralph's previously published books and will be releasing his unpublished manuscripts, too.

I really sense Irma's spirit as Ralph's work is finally getting a second life. She would be so pleased know that a new generation of readers is about to discover his Hardman novels and I'm certain that the first publication of his long-lost manuscripts will bring a new, greater appreciation for his talent.

RICHARD A. MOORE is the author of three novels and various short stories published by Ellery Queen, Alfred Hitchcock and other mystery magazines and anthologies. A former reporter and retired public relations executive, he lives in Virginia, happily writing full time.

ABOUT THE AUTHOR

Ralph Dennis isn't a household name...but he should be. He is widely considered among crime writers as a master of the genre, denied the recognition he deserved because his twelve *Hardman* books, which are beloved and highly sought-after collectables now, were poorly packaged in the 1970s by Popular Library as a cheap men's action-adventure paperbacks with numbered titles.

Even so, some top critics saw past the cheesy covers and noticed that he was producing work as good as John D. MacDonald, Raymond Chandler, Chester Himes, Dashiell Hammett, and Ross MacDonald.

The *New York Times* praised the *Hardman* novels for "expert writing, plotting, and an unusual degree of sensitivity. Dennis has mastered the genre and supplied top entertainment." The *Philadelphia Daily News* proclaimed *Hardman* "the best series around, but they've got such terrible covers..."

Unfortunately, Popular Library didn't take the hint and continued to present the series like hack work, dooming the novels to a short shelf-life and obscurity...except among generations of crime writers, like novelist Joe R. Lansdale (the *Hap & Leonard* series) and screenwriter Shane Black (the *Lethal Weapon* movies), who've kept Dennis' legacy alive through word-of-mouth and by acknowledging his influence on their stellar work.

Ralph Dennis wrote three other novels that were published outside of the *Hardman* series—*Atlanta, Deadman's Game* and *MacTaggart's War*—but he wasn't able to reach the wide audience, or gain the critical acclaim, that he deserved during his lifetime.

He was born in 1931 in Sumter, South Carolina, and received a masters degree from University of North Carolina, where he later taught film and television writing after serving a stint in the Navy. At the time of his death in 1988, he was working at a bookstore in Atlanta and had a file cabinet full of unpublished novels.

Brash Books will be releasing the entire *Hardman* series, his three other published novels, and his long-lost manuscripts.

Made in the USA
Monee, IL
06 February 2024